"I'm not a callous jerk, no matter what kind of first impression I gave you."

She patted his hand, which still rested on the table in front of her. "You still have a chance to redeem yourself."

By the time the waiter brought the check, Graham felt almost comfortable with her. He debated asking her out for a real date, but decided to wait. He'd be sure to see her again; the case gave him a good excuse to do so.

He walked her to her Jeep and lingered while she found her keys and unlocked the car door. "Here's my personal cell." He wrote the number on the back of his business card and handed it to her. "Call me anytime."

"About the case—or just to talk?" Her tone was teasing.

"Either. Maybe you'd like to give me your number?"

She smiled and opened her purse. But she never had a chance to write down her number. The loud crack of gunshots shattered the afternoon silence. Her screams rang in Graham's ears as he pushed her to the ground.

LAWMAN PROTECTION

CINDI MYERS

For Mike

ISBN-13: 978-0-373-74899-0

Lawman Protection

This edition published by arrangement with Harlequin Books S.A.

For questions and comments about the quality of this book, please contact us at CustomerService@Harlequin.com.

Printed in U.S.A.

Cindi Myers is an author of more than fifty novels. When she's not crafting new romance plots, she enjoys skiing, gardening, cooking, crafting and daydreaming. A lover of small-town life, she lives with her husband and two spoiled dogs in the Colorado mountains.

Books by Cindi Myers

The Ranger Brigade series

The Guardian
Lawman Protection

HARLEQUIN INTRIGUE

Rocky Mountain Revenge
Rocky Mountain Rescue

HARLEQUIN HEARTWARMING

Her Cowboy Soldier
What She'd Do for Love

Visit the Author Profile page at Harlequin.com for more titles.

CAST OF CHARACTERS

Graham Ellison—Captain of The Ranger Brigade, this FBI agent has little time to waste with the journalists who want to criticize his methods and interfere with his pursuit of justice. He's used to being in command and doesn't know how to handle an independent reporter he can't control.

Emma Wade—The reporter has devoted her career to seeking justice for crime victims. The tall, curvy redhead intimidates some men, so she appreciates the powerful Ranger captain who is willing to stand up to and spar with her. But she won't let her attraction to Graham keep her from prodding him to do everything in his power to find a missing TV anchor.

Lauren Starling—The popular prime-time anchor for a Denver news channel has been missing ever since her car was found abandoned at an overlook in Black Canyon in Gunnison National Park a month ago. With no evidence of foul play and rumors that Lauren suffered from depression in the wake of a divorce and trouble on the job, the Rangers fear she may have come to the park to commit suicide.

Bobby Pace—The private pilot, anxious to pay the bills piling up from his son's cancer treatments, flew for anyone who would pay him. Working for the wrong client may have cost him his life.

Richard Prentice—The infamous billionaire has made a career out of manipulating state and federal government officials, but The Ranger Brigade refuses to bend to his will. Is Prentice the power behind the recent crime wave, or are his criticisms of the Rangers justified?

Valentina Ferrari—The part-time model and daughter of the Venezuelan ambassador to the US has been linked romantically with Richard Prentice in the press.

Senator Peter Mattheson—The senator from Colorado is leading the charge to disband The Ranger Brigade.

The Ranger Brigade—An interagency task force of law enforcement officers charged with fighting crime on public lands in southwest Colorado, including Black Canyon in Gunnison National Park, Curecanti Wilderness Area and Gunnison Gorge Wilderness Area.

Chapter One

"Would you rather face down half a dozen reporters at a press conference, or shoot it out with drug runners in the backcountry?"

FBI Captain Graham Ellison gave his questioner, Montrose County sheriff's deputy Lance Carpenter, a sour look. "Is that a trick question? At least with the drug runners I've got a fair chance. It doesn't matter what I say at these press conferences. The media puts the spin on it they want."

"If the questions get too tough, just look menacing and tell them the safety of local citizens is your primary concern." Carpenter clapped Graham on the back. "You'll do great."

Graham eyed the crowd of reporters, cameramen and news trucks waiting in the parking lot outside the trailer that served as headquarters for The Ranger Brigade—the nickname given to an interagency task force addressing crime on public lands in southwest Colorado. "The safety of citizens *is* my primary concern," he said. "Or one of them. I have a lot of concerns—and I don't need reporters telling me how to do my job, or wasting my time listing all the ways I'm doing it wrong."

"I don't think you've got any choice in the matter this time." Lance studied the gathering over Graham's shoulder. "Prentice and Senator Mattheson forced your hand."

Graham let out a low growl and shifted his focus to the newspaper that lay open on his desk. Twin headlines summed up his predicament: Mattheson Calls for Dismantling Task Force read one. Prentice Readies for Battle declared the other. Peter Mattheson, senator from Colorado, was on a crusade to "get the feds out of local law enforcement business" and "stop wasting money on federal boondoggles."

Richard Prentice, a billionaire who'd made a career out of buying up environmentally or historically valuable properties, then blackmailing the federal government into paying top dollar to save the parcels, had filed a lawsuit to force local authorities to allow him to develop property he owned at the entrance to the Black Canyon of the Gunnison National Park.

Graham's bosses in Washington had "suggested" he hold a press conference to address both these issues. "We'd better get out there before they start making stuff up," Graham said. He straightened his shoulders, opened the door and stepped out into a hail of shouted questions.

"Captain Ellison, have you spoken with Richard Prentice?"

"Captain Ellison, has the death of Raul Meredes slowed drug trafficking in the area?"

"Captain Ellison, how do you respond to Senator Mattheson's criticisms of the task force?"

Graham stood on the top step of the trailer and glowered at the gathered media. Flashes around him let him know his scowling face would be in newspapers all over the region tomorrow. More than one news account had described him as "a big bear of a man." He hoped this time they'd look at him and think "grizzly." He scanned the crowd for a familiar face, some reporter he knew who'd let him ease into the grilling with a softball question.

A cameraman moved to one side, adjusting his angle, and a woman took advantage of the opening to step forward. Digital recorder in one hand, notebook in the other, she was clearly a reporter, but not one Graham had seen before. He wouldn't forget a figure like hers. She was tall, with a generous chest and curvy hips, a wild tumble of strawberry blond hair and full lips in a perfect pink bow of a mouth. Her eyes were hidden by fashionably large sunglasses, but he had no doubt she was looking right at him. And frankly, he couldn't stop staring at her. Forget the fragile, stick-figure women so popular in magazines and on television—here was a real-live, flesh-and-blood goddess. Here was a woman he could embrace without crushing, one he could kiss without getting a crick in his back, one…

"Captain Ellison, what are you doing about the disappearance of Lauren Starling?" the woman asked, her voice husky and deep, carrying easily even in the crowd.

At her words, his fantasy vanished like a puff of smoke. She wasn't the perfect woman—she was a reporter. And judging from the frown on her face, she didn't think much of him. "So far it has not been determined that Ms. Starling is a missing person, or that she is, in fact, missing in our territory. We are working with the Denver police to try to determine her whereabouts."

"You don't think finding her car abandoned in the National Park, not a half mile from where we're standing right now, points to some connection between her failing to show up for work two weeks ago and 'your territory?'"

Lauren Starling was the popular nightly news anchor at Denver's number two news station. Three weeks ago, she'd failed to return from a few days' vacation and park rangers had discovered her car abandoned at an overlook in Black Canyon of the Gunnison National Park. "Denver police are in charge of that investigation and they are keeping us apprised," Graham said. What he wished he could say was that, for all he or anyone else knew, Lauren Starling was in Mexico with a secret boyfriend. "At this point we have no evidence of foul play."

Twin lines, like the number eleven, formed between the woman's eyes and her mouth turned down in disapproval. Clearly, she didn't think much of his answer. Too bad. He had bigger things to worry about than one woman who the Denver cops had hinted was more than a little flighty. His officers were keeping their eyes open for any sign of Ms. Starling, but he wasn't losing sleep over her.

"Captain, did the death of Raul Meredes put an end to drug trafficking on public lands?"

A reedy man Graham recognized as being from the local county paper asked the question. Meredes had been in charge of a large marijuana-growing and human-trafficking operation based in the National Park. Identifying him as a key figure in the recent crime spree had been the task force's biggest achievement thus far. Unfortunately, Meredes had been murdered before they could question him. The crime rate in the area had dipped following his demise, but Graham sensed the lull represented only a marshaling of resources, in preparation for another surge.

"Mr. Meredes played a major role in the crimes going on in this area," Graham said. "But we don't believe he was the one supplying the money and man power for the operation. We're still trying to track down that individual."

"Do you think Richard Prentice has any connection to criminal activity in the park?"

Graham wasn't sure who asked that question; it came from the back of the crowd. Had someone leaked the task force's suspicions, or had Prentice himself sent someone to test how much the Rangers knew?

"We have no reason to believe Mr. Prentice has anything to do with the crimes in the park," he said. Prentice was a jerk and a thorn in the side of federal and state officials in general, but being nasty and unpleasant didn't make a man a criminal. Which didn't mean the task force wasn't watching him very closely. But Prentice had a lot of money, and a lot of lawyers, so they had to tread carefully, which meant not airing their suspicions to the press.

"What do you think of his plans to build a housing development at the entrance to the park?" asked the stringer for the Telluride paper.

"I don't think my opinion on the matter is relevant," Graham said. "I have bigger things to focus on at the moment than Mr. Prentice's battle for public opinion." He glanced at his watch; he'd been standing up here only five minutes. How much longer before he could make his escape?

"What do you have to say to Senator Mattheson's charges that a multi-agency task force is an ineffective and expensive way to address problems better handled by local law enforcement?" The question came from the female reporter. She'd removed her sunglasses to reveal hazel eyes fringed with long, dark lashes. But there was no warmth in those eyes for him.

"I would remind Senator Mattheson that local law enforcement requested help from the federal government in addressing the multiple crimes that seemed to be originating from federal lands," Graham said. "Law enforcement on public land has always been the purview of federal park rangers and the various federal agencies who oversee various federal regulations, from ATF to Border Patrol. This task force brings members of those agencies together to pool resources and provide a more focused approach to addressing crime in a vast and largely unpoliced area."

"But in three months you've only made one arrest, and you're no closer to identifying the person responsible for this crime wave," she said.

"Real life isn't like television, where every case is wrapped up in an hour," he said, barely reining in his annoyance.

"And you don't think Lauren Starling's disappearance has any connection to the other crimes within the park?" she asked, recorder extended toward him.

"I believe I've addressed the question already." He turned away, aware of her gaze boring into him.

"Captain?"

He turned and found Lance, cell phone in hand. "I think you'd better take this call," the deputy said. He handed the phone to Graham, then stepped forward to address the reporters. "We're going to have to wrap this up now," he said. "Thank you all for coming."

At first, Graham thought the sheriff's deputy had manufactured the call, as a ruse to end the press conference early. *Points for him*, Graham thought as he turned his back to the reporters and spoke into the phone. "Ellison here."

"Captain, Randall here." Randall Knightbridge was the Bureau of Land Management's representative on the team. His voice was strained, putting Graham on alert; this was no fake call.

"What is it, Randall?"

"Marco and I were patrolling in the Curecanti Recreation Area and we came upon a plane wreck. It looks recent—within the last day or so." Marco Cruz was with the DEA, probably the best tracker on the task force—well, the best, except for Randall's dog, Lotte. "A Beechcraft Bonanza," Randall continued. "One casualty—the pilot."

"Give me your coordinates and I'll send a team right away." Graham pulled a notepad and pen from the front pocket of his uniform shirt.

Randall rattled off the GPS coordinates.

"You probably want to come with the team," he said.

Graham tucked the notebook back into his pocket and glanced over his shoulder at the departing press. The curvy blonde was trailing the pack, headed toward a red SUV parked at the far end of the lot. For a moment he was transfixed on the tantalizing sway of her backside as she moved away from him. Too bad she was a reporter...

"Captain?" Randall's voice recalled him from his fantasies.

"I'm here. What were you saying?"

"I said, there's some interesting cargo here you're definitely going to want to see."

EMMA WADE STARED at the captain's back through the windshield of her Jeep Wrangler—broad shoulders, muscular arms and yes, a very nice rear end. In other circumstances, he was exactly the kind of guy she'd go for—big enough that she wouldn't feel like an elephant next to him. Strong. Intelligent. Too bad he was a jerk.

He finished one call and immediately made two more, then barked something at the sheriff's deputy at his side. She was too far away to hear the words, but the tension in his expression and body language made her sit up straighter. Something was up.

Graham Ellison and the deputy headed for a black-and-white FJ Cruiser parked on the side of the task force trailer. Emma fastened her seat belt and started her vehicle. The press conference had been a bust as far as gathering any new information, but she didn't have to go home empty-handed. Wherever the captain was headed, maybe there was a story there.

He could refuse to answer her questions at the news conference, but he couldn't keep her off public land. Fresh anger rose at the memory of his easy dismissal of the idea that Lauren Starling might be a concern of his precious task force. The police had had the same attitude ten years ago, when Sherry had turned up missing. The next thing Emma knew, she'd been attending her sister's funeral. She gripped the steering wheel of the Jeep until her knuckles ached. Captain Ellison might think he'd heard the last from her about Lauren, but he was wrong. She wouldn't let another family suffer the way hers had if she could help it.

She eased off the accelerator, letting the Cruiser get farther ahead. Unpaved roads made following easy—she could track the plume of dust that rose behind the speeding vehicle, her own vehicle hidden by the dirty cloud.

When the Cruiser's tracks turned off the road, headed across the prairie, she hesitated only a fraction of a second before following. The Jeep bounced over the rough terrain, rattling her teeth, and she prayed she wouldn't blow a tire. They were headed away from the canyon that gave the park its name, across an expanse of rocky ground pocked with sagebrush and piñon trees, deep into the roadless wilderness area where few people ventured. All that largely unpatrolled public land had proved attractive to the criminals who'd taken advantage of sheltered canyons and abandoned ranch buildings to plant marijuana, manufacture methamphetamine and smuggle people and illegal goods. Hence the need for the task force, though public opinion wasn't convinced that the influx of law enforcement had been much of a crime deterrent.

The dust was beginning to settle around two black-and-white Cruisers by the time Emma parked the Jeep a few yards behind them. As she climbed out of her vehicle, she focused on the mass of wreckage behind the cops: the tail and one wing of a small plane pointed skyward, the nose crumpled against the prairie. She took a couple of pictures with her digital camera then, aware of at least two cops glaring at her, strode forward with all the confidence of a journalist who knows she has every right to be where these men didn't want her.

"Stop right there, ma'am." A rangy officer in a long-sleeved brown shirt, khakis and a buff Stetson stepped out to meet her. A blond-and-black police dog stalked at his side, golden eyes fixed on her.

"Hello, Officer. I'm Emma Wade, from the *Denver Post*."

"You need to turn around and leave, Ms. Wade. This is a crime scene."

"Oh?" She directed her gaze over his shoulder, to where the captain and two other officers were huddled at the door of the crashed plane. "What kind of crime? Was the plane carrying drugs? Illegal aliens? Some other contraband? Did anyone survive the crash? Do you know who the plane belongs to?" She took out her reporter's notebook, pen poised. She didn't really expect him to answer any of her queries, but sometimes interrogating men who were more used to assuming the role of interrogator yielded interesting results.

He glanced over his shoulder toward the plane, then back at her, his expression tense. "No comment," he said.

"Then I'd better talk to someone else." She started forward, but he put out his arm to stop her.

"You really need to leave," he said.

"After I've driven all the way out here?" She folded her arms across her chest. "I'll stay."

"Then you'll have to wait over there." He motioned in the direction of her Jeep.

Clearly, he wasn't going to let her any closer. Better to wait him out. "All right." She replaced the notebook in her purse. "Tell Captain Ellison I have some questions for him when he's finished."

She turned and walked back to her vehicle, not in any hurry. Once there, she rummaged in the glove compartment until she found a pair of binoculars. She leaned against the Jeep and trained the binocs on the wreckage.

Debris littered the area around the crash—chunks of fiberglass and metal, a tire, a plastic cup, the remains of a wooden crate. She focused in on the crate and made out the words *Fragile* and *Property of*— Property of whom?

She scanned to the right of the crate and froze when she found herself looking into a pair of eyes the color of hot fudge, underneath craggy brows.

Angry brown eyes, she corrected herself, that belonged to Captain Graham Ellison. He glared directly at her and she gasped and drew back as he stalked toward her.

By the time he reached her Jeep, she'd lowered the binoculars and was doing her best not to look intimidated, though the site of the big bear of a man glaring at her was enough to make a guilty person tremble.

But she hadn't done anything wrong, she reminded herself. "Hello, Captain," she said. "What can you tell me about this plane crash?"

"Why did you follow me out here?" he asked.

"I'm a reporter. It's what I do— I track down stories." She took out her notebook and pen. "When do you think the plane crashed? It looks recent, considering the broken tree limbs are still green, and the scar in the earth looks fresh."

"So now you're an expert?" Irritation radiated from him like heat, but she was no longer nervous or afraid. His intensity excited her, both professionally and—she wasn't going to analyze this now, only note that it was true—personally. Being attracted to Captain Ellison might complicate things a little, but it didn't mean she couldn't do her job.

"Not an expert," she said. "But I've been a crime reporter for a while now. Who does the plane belong to? Do you know?"

"Whoever he is, he's dead."

"Oh." Her pen faltered, leaving a scribble on the notebook. "I suppose it would be difficult for anyone to survive a crash like that."

"Oh, he survived," Ellison said. "Then someone put a bullet in him."

She swallowed hard. She didn't like this aspect of her work, dealing with violence. But finding justice for victims often began with exposing the particulars of the crime. "How was he killed?"

"He was shot. In the chest."

"Do you know who he is?"

"Who do you work for, again?"

"The *Denver Post*. I'm with the Western Slope Bureau." She *was* the Western Slope Bureau. While she wrote stories about everything from local festivals to water rights, she specialized in crime reporting. The attempted arrest and subsequent murder of Raul Meredes had focused her attention on The Ranger Brigade—a romantic name for a disparate collection of officers from all the federal law enforcement agencies.

"If you're so interested in this story, maybe you'd like a closer look." He took her arm and pulled her toward the plane.

She didn't protest. Clearly, he wanted to shock her, to frighten her even, but she'd seen death before. Whatever that plane held, she'd study it objectively and write about it later. She'd show the captain she was tougher than he thought. She wouldn't be bullied or intimidated just because he didn't like the job she was doing.

The pilot slumped sideways in his seat, safety belt still fastened, his shirt stained brown with dried blood. Flies buzzed around him, and she swallowed hard against the sickly stench that rose to greet her. "Recognize him?" the captain asked. He still held on to her arm, as if he feared she might bolt.

She started to look away, to shake her head, but that was what he wanted, wasn't it? For her to be horrified and repulsed. She straightened her shoulders and forced herself to lean closer, to study the dead man, whose face was turned away from her. When she did so, true horror washed over her. She fought to breathe, and tears stung her eyes.

"What is it?" the captain shook her. "You're not going to be sick, are you?"

She shook her head and wrenched away from him. "I…I do know him," she gasped, then covered her mouth with her hand, fighting nausea.

"Who is he?" Ellison demanded.

"His name is Bobby Pace. I… He… We were dating. I went out with him two nights ago."

Chapter Two

The stricken look on Emma Wade's face made Graham feel like the lowest form of jerk. He'd been furious with her for nosing her way into his investigation, but that didn't give him the right to treat her so cruelly. "Come on." He put his arm around her and turned her away from the sight of the dead man. "I'll take you back to headquarters and we can talk there."

"I'll be fine." She tried to rally, but fresh tears streamed down her face.

"I'll have one of the officers bring your Jeep," he said. "You come with me."

She didn't protest as he helped her into the Cruiser. "Bring her Jeep with you when you come back to headquarters," he told Randall, then he climbed into the driver's seat.

Neither of them said a word as the vehicle bounced over the rough terrain. He kept stealing glances at her. She'd stopped crying, and was staring out the windshield with the look of someone who wasn't seeing what was right in front of her. Even in her grief, she was beautiful; he fought against the desire to hold and comfort her. She was a reporter, and a potential witness in his case. He needed to fight his attraction to her and keep his distance.

At headquarters, he led her into his cramped office at the back of the trailer and moved a stack of binders to make room for her in one of the two folding chairs in front of his desk. The administrative assistant who helped deal with the mountains of paperwork the job entailed was off today, so they had the building to themselves, at least until the rest of the team got back from the crash site. He opened a bottle of water from the case that sat in the corner and handed it to her, then pulled the other folding chair alongside her. "First, I apologize for being such a jerk back there," he said. "I get a little...*intense*, sometimes."

"And you don't like the press." Her eyes met his over the top of the water bottle. They were the green-gold of dragonflies, he thought, fringed with gold-tipped lashes.

Focus, he reminded himself. "The press sometimes makes my job more difficult."

"And men like you make *my* job more difficult." Amusement glinted in those beautiful eyes, and he had to look away.

"What can you tell me about the man in the plane?" he asked. "Was he the pilot?"

"Bobby was a pilot. I never saw his plane, but I know he owned a Bonanza."

"You and he had been dating?" Some emotion he didn't want to look at too closely—jealousy?—pinched at him and he pushed it away. "For how long?"

"We only went out a few times. We weren't lovers, just friends. He was having a hard time and needed someone to talk to."

"What do you mean, having a hard time?"

"His little boy is sick, and needs a lot of expensive care. Bobby was worried about money—that's the reason he took the job with Richard Prentice, even though he couldn't stand the guy."

"He worked for Richard Prentice?"

She nodded. "That's how we met. I wrote a profile of Prentice for the *Post* last year. Bobby was kind of like a chauffeur—he piloted his Bonanza, or sometimes he flew a plane Prentice owned. He was on call to take Prentice wherever he needed to go."

"When you saw him two nights ago, did he say anything about doing a job for Prentice the next day, or the next?"

"No. We didn't talk about work. And he didn't just fly for Prentice. He worked for anybody who wanted to hire his plane. He taught flying lessons, too." She set the still-full water bottle on the desk and leaned toward him. "What happened? Did the plane crash because he was shot, or did that happen after they were on the ground?"

"We don't know, though someone would have to be pretty stupid to shoot the pilot while they were still in the air."

"You're sure there was a passenger?"

"We're not sure about anything. But someone shot your friend, and someone took the cargo that was in the plane. And we found fresh tracks that looked like a truck or another big vehicle pulled up alongside the wreckage." He clamped his mouth shut. He was telling her too much.

"I saw the busted-up crate," she said. "What was in it?"

"We don't know that, either." Though Marco Cruz, the DEA agent who'd been patrolling with Randall, had recognized the markings on the crate.

"Do you think this is connected with Richard Prentice?" she asked. "Is he running a smuggling operation?"

"We don't know. How well do you know him? You said you wrote a profile for the paper?"

"I spent two weeks visiting his home and shadowing him as he conducted business. He was charming. Arrogant, but when you have as much money as he does, maybe it comes with the territory."

So she thought Prentice was charming? The idea annoyed him, probably more than it should, but he wasn't going to waste any more time playing the polite card. "I'll need you to tell me everything you know about Richard Prentice. And I want to see all your notes, recordings and any other material you collected while researching your article."

"I'm not one of your officers who you can boss around, Captain," she said. "If you really want that information, you can get a subpoena." She stood, her face flushed, eyes practically snapping with fury. "And if you want to know about Richard Prentice, read the article." She stalked out of his office, slamming the door hard behind her.

He stared after her, stomach churning. So much for his attempt to not be a jerk around her. But the thought of her and that arrogant billionaire…

"Captain! Wait 'til you hear this." Marco

Cruz, trailed by Randall Knightbridge, burst into the headquarters trailer. Lean and muscular, with skin the color of honey, Marco was the epitome of the strong, silent type. But at the moment, his face was more animated than Graham could remember ever seeing it.

"What's up?" he asked, rising to meet them.

"I made some calls to some people I know," Marco said. "I think my hunch about what was in that crate was right."

"So what was in it?" Graham had no patience for top secret time-wasting, not when the agencies were supposed to be working together.

"I thought the crate looked just like the ones the military uses to ship Hellfire missiles. My sources in the army tell me they've had a few come up missing the last couple of years."

"What, they just lost track?" Graham asked.

"That's what I said," Randall said. "But I guess people steal them to sell on the black market."

"So what was a Hellfire missile doing in that plane?" Graham asked. "Provided that's what was really in that box."

"Hellfire missiles are what they use to arm unmanned drones," Marco said.

The hairs on the back of Graham's neck stood up. "Anybody with enough money can buy a drone from a private company. It's not illegal."

"But only someone with a Hellfire missile can arm that drone," Marco said.

"Who around here owns a drone?" Graham asked.

Marco nodded. "That's what we need to find out. And fast."

FORGET GRAHAM ELLISON, Emma told herself as she unlocked the door to her house in a quiet suburb on Montrose's south side. She didn't need him to get to the bottom of this story. Safely inside, she dumped her purse and the day's mail on the kitchen table.

"Meow!" A silver-gray tabby emerged from the bedroom and leaned against her ankles.

"Hello, Janey, darling." Emma bent and scooped the cat into her arms. As she rubbed a finger beneath the furry chin Janey—for Jane Austen—purred loudly.

"How was your day?" Emma asked. "I had to deal with the most frustrating man."

"Meow!" Janey said—though whether in sympathy, or simply because she wanted to be fed, Emma couldn't say.

But she opened a can of Salmon Supreme and dumped it into Janey's dish, then poured herself a glass of wine and sat at the table to try to organize her notes. She didn't have that much, but she had enough to write a story about the plane crash. For a painful moment the image of Bobby's lifeless body slumped in the pilot's seat of his destroyed plane flashed into her mind and she felt a sharp pang of grief for her friend.

She swallowed her tears and opened her notebook. All the more reason to do everything she could to find his killer. Bobby had been a great guy—not a man she could fall in love with, but a good friend, and he deserved better.

Her doorbell rang, the loud chimes startling her. She hurried to the door and checked the peephole, and sucked in a breath when she saw Graham Ellison standing there. He was still in uniform, but he held a large bouquet of flowers in his hand, wrapped in green tissue paper.

She unlocked the door and opened it. "Captain, what are you doing here?" she asked.

"It seems like I'm always apologizing to you," he said. "We got off on the wrong foot. Can we try again?"

She regarded him warily, trying hard not to notice how he towered over her, or how his shoulders were almost wide enough to fill the doorway. A man who made her feel dainty was a rarity, and she usually liked to savor the experience. But she had trouble relaxing around Captain Ellison. "Why should I give you another chance?" she asked.

"Because we both want to find out who killed your friend."

It was the one answer that was sure to sway her. She held the door open wider. "Come in."

He moved past her into the foyer, and handed her the flowers. "Peace offering," he said.

"Come in here." She led the way into the kitchen, and motioned to the table. "I was just going over my notes." She found a vase in a cabinet and filled it at the sink.

"I'm not going to make the mistake of asking to see them."

She flushed. "I don't like being ordered around. Also—I have my own system for organizing my research material. It's messy and it probably wouldn't make sense to anyone else."

"I shouldn't have barked at you like you were one of my junior officers."

She arranged the flowers in the vase and set it on the counter, then looked him in the eye, ignoring the way her heart sped up when she did so. "What is it about me you don't like?" she asked. "Is it just because I'm a reporter?

Because we're on the same side here. I want to know who killed Bobby, and I want to see them brought to justice."

He grimaced, as if in pain. "You've got it all wrong. Our problems aren't because I don't like you—they're because I'm so attracted to you."

Now her heart was really racing, and she felt as if she'd swallowed battling hummingbirds. So she wasn't the only one who'd noticed the heat between them. "I'm intrigued. Tell me more."

He looked around the apartment, everywhere but at her. His gaze finally focused on the cat, who had finished eating and was meticulously grooming herself. "When I saw you in that crowd of reporters, I had a hard time not staring." He hazarded a glance her way. "Is this going to get me into trouble?"

"That depends on your definition of trouble."

He shoved both hands in his pockets. "We're both professionals. Maybe we should keep it that way."

"Or maybe we should be more honest." She stepped out from behind the kitchen counter, moving toward him. "I'm an adult. I think I can handle my job and my personal life without ruining either."

"What are you saying?"

"I'm saying I'm attracted to you, too, Captain. It takes a special man to appreciate a woman like me."

His gaze swept over her like a caress. "Then those other men are fools."

She laughed. "Maybe. But some men don't know how to handle a woman who's five-eleven and probably outweighs them. I'm no delicate flower."

"I'm not interested in flowers." His gaze drifted to her cleavage. She had plenty of that. And an ample backside. He wouldn't be the first guy to appreciate her killer curves, even if the women in fashion magazines never looked like her.

"So did you come here this afternoon to ask me out?" she asked.

"No. I came to ask for your help. You know a lot more about Richard Prentice than I do. Maybe you can give me some insight."

"Richard Prentice?" The mention of the billionaire surprised her. "Do you think he's behind Bobby's death?"

"We don't know. Your friend worked for him, so that seems the most logical place to start our investigation."

He still wouldn't look her in the eye, a sure sign he was holding something back. "You're not telling me everything," she said.

"Why focus on Prentice? Do you think he's connected to other crimes in the park?"

"I'd rather you tell me what you think—and what you know—about Prentice."

She considered the question for a moment, sorting through her impressions of the billionaire. "He pretty much hates the federal government, but you already know that," she said. "He's made a career of forcing the government's hand and of trying to circumvent regulations he sees as controlling and unjust. But he's never broken the law."

"Never that anyone can prove."

"But you think he has now? Why? How?"

Graham shook his head. "I have no proof that Mr. Prentice has anything to do with any crime—his only connection is that the dead pilot was known to have worked for him."

"But you have your suspicions."

His silence was as good as a confirmation. "I understand why you won't say anything more," she said. "And I wouldn't write anything about Mr. Prentice without a lot of proof to back it up—he can afford very good lawyers and we both know he's not afraid to use them. But anything you can tell me I'll keep in confidence until it's appropriate to write about it."

The line of his jaw tightened, but he gave a

single nod. "I can't tell you everything I know about the case," he said. "But I will say—off the record—that the cargo we think was in that plane could be very dangerous, and it's definitely illegal."

"Will you tell me more when you can?"

He hesitated. "When I can, yes."

"Then I'll tell you what I know about Richard Prentice, even though I don't see how it can help."

He took his hands out of his pockets, and some of the tension went out of his shoulders. "Good. Why don't we discuss this over dinner?"

"Is this a date?"

He flushed. "No. Yes. Why don't we call it dinner and see what happens after that?"

EMMA INSISTED ON driving her Jeep to the restaurant, with Graham following in his Cruiser. He'd do whatever it took to put her at ease, though he wasn't used to yielding control. The little Italian bistro occupied an old house off a side street, and at this time of day they were the only customers, but the owners seemed to know Emma and greeted her warmly. "I just took some lasagna out of the oven," the woman, who looked more like Sophia Loren than an Italian grandmother, said.

"And we have a new wine you should try," her husband, a short, burly man added.

Emma looked at Graham. "Does that sound good to you?"

His stomach growled, and he realized he hadn't had anything but coffee since breakfast. "It sounds great."

The couple left them alone in a secluded booth and Graham studied Emma across the table, vowing that he wouldn't press her for information, even though he was dying to know her impressions of Richard Prentice—and what her relationship with the billionaire might have been. She'd insisted on changing before they went out, and instead of the jeans and boots she'd worn earlier, she'd put on a long dress made out of some light fabric that clung to her curves. A colorful scarf around her shoulders brought out the green in her eyes. She looked soft and sexy and too distracting for him to be comfortable. He still wasn't sure how he felt about her suggestion that they explore their mutual attraction. Getting involved with a reporter struck him as one of the worst ideas he'd ever had.

But if the reporter was a beautiful woman...

"My editor at the *Post* wanted a story on Richard Prentice after his run-in with the county officials here over his attempts to force the federal government to buy the land he owns near the park entrance," she said after their host, Ray, brought their wine. "I approached Prentice with the angle that this would be a chance for him to tell his side of the story. He ended up inviting me to visit his ranch and shadow him for a couple of weeks."

"Maybe he wanted you close, where he could keep an eye on you." His fingers tightened on the stem of the wineglass as he thought of how close Prentice had probably wanted to be to her. As close as Graham himself wanted to be.

"Maybe. But it worked in my favor. I met the people who worked for him, saw how he lived."

"What did you think?"

A smile tugged at the corners of her mouth. "You really should read the article."

"I will, but give me your impressions now."

"All right." She spread her hands flat on the table in front of her. She wore rings on one thumb and three fingers of each hand. Her nails were polished a shell pink, the manicure fresh. "First of all, he's smarter than you probably think. A genius, even. He can rattle off phone numbers of almost everyone he's ever called, remember minute details about things that happened years ago—he practically has a photographic memory."

"Smart people can still do dumb things."

"Yes. And he does have a weakness—because he's very smart, he views everyone else as dumb. That kind of arrogance leads him to underestimate his opponents sometimes."

The woman, Lola, brought two plates loaded with thick slabs of fragrant lasagna, accompanied by buttered and seasoned zucchini. "This looks amazing," Graham said as he spread a napkin in his lap.

"It is." Lola beamed. "My special recipe."

"It really is divine," Emma said. She slid a forkful into her mouth and moaned softly.

The sound made Graham's mouth go dry. He shifted to accommodate his sudden arousal, and took a long sip of wine. When was the last time a woman had affected him this way? Maybe when he was a teenager—twenty years ago. "What kind of people does Prentice hang out with?" he asked. *Focus on the case.*

"All kinds. Politicians. Foreign businesspeople. Fashion models. Celebrities. Lobbyists. People who want favors. People he can order around. He's not the kind of man who has close friends, though, just a lot of contacts and acquaintances."

"Any romantic interests?"

She shook her head. "He's been photographed with a lot of beautiful women at various events, but he treats them like accessories—necessary to his image, but there's no real attachment there. He likes women, but they're not an obsession. And in case you're wondering, he was a perfect gentleman around me."

Neither *perfect* nor *gentleman* fit his impression of Prentice, but he was relieved to know the man hadn't taken a personal interest in Emma. "How did he get all that money he has?"

"He was vague about that. Some of it he inherited. He owns a lot of different companies. He's sort of known for running competitors out of business, and for buying up marginal concerns and selling off their assets. As you might have gathered, he has no qualms about using people or situations for his own gain."

"He clearly enjoys sticking it to the government."

"Definitely. Believe it or not, he sees himself as a kind of champion, fighting against the feds. And there are people who look up to him for that."

"Even if it means destroying historic landmarks or using public land for private gain?"

She nodded. "I met some of his fans—everybody from property rights lobbyists to extremist groups who believe everything the government does is wrong."

"So if he wanted to do something illegal, he could probably find people to help him."

"I'm sure. And they don't have to be fans of his—he has enough money to pay anyone to do what he wants. For some people that's enough."

He had enough money to buy a drone and a black-market missile to arm it. And people who'd cheer him on as he did so. "I'll probably have more questions for you later, but right now, let's change the subject to something less grim," he said. "Why did you decide to be a reporter?"

She laughed, and the sound sent a tremor through his middle. "You don't have to sound so disgusted. I'm not an ax murderer."

He winced. "Sorry. Let's just say a lot of my interactions with the press haven't been positive."

"I can't imagine." Suppressed laughter again.

Point taken. "So I'm not Mr. Personality. But I really do want to know what drew you to journalism."

She sat back and took a deep breath, as if

bracing herself for an ordeal. "All right, I'll tell you. When I was nineteen, a freshman in college, my older sister disappeared. She was a nurse, working nights at a hospital. She got off her shift early one morning and was never seen or heard from again."

He felt the pain behind her words, despite her calm demeanor. "How awful for your family," he said, the words completely inadequate.

She nodded. "Sherry had left once before without telling the rest of us—she'd run off to Vegas with a guy she was dating for a wild weekend. At first the police suspected a repeat of that caper. We tried to tell them that this time was different, but they wouldn't listen. They didn't take the case seriously until we went to the newspapers. A reporter took an interest in the case and helped us. Eventually, the police found her body, not far from the hospital. She'd been murdered. They never found her killer."

He reached across the table and took her hand. "I'm sorry."

"Thank you." She withdrew her hand and sipped wine. "Anyway, that reporter inspired me. I wanted to help others the way she helped our family. Sometimes that means riding the police—reminding them to do their job."

"Those questions you asked about Lauren Starling." Understanding dawned.

She nodded. "She's another woman who's gone missing, and no one is doing anything about it."

"We are keeping our eyes open for any sign of her. But we don't have anything else to go on."

"I'm still trying to find out more about her and the case," she said.

"If you learn anything, let me know," he said. "I'm not a callous jerk, no matter what kind of first impression I gave you."

She patted his hand, which still rested on the table in front of her. "You still have a chance to redeem yourself."

They finished the meal over espresso and small talk about each other's background. He told her about growing up in a military family, playing football, then joining the marines and eventually moving into law enforcement with the FBI. "No wife or family?" she asked.

"I was married once, but it didn't work out. I guess I'm one of those men who's married to his work. No kids. What about you?"

She shook her head. "I was engaged once, but we both thought better of it."

By the time Ray brought the check, Graham felt almost comfortable with her. He debated asking her out for a real date, but decided to wait. He'd be sure to see her again; the case gave him a good excuse to do so. No need to rush things and risk screwing up.

He walked her to her Jeep and lingered while she found her keys and unlocked the car door. "Here's my personal cell." He wrote the number on the back of his business card and handed it to her. "Call me anytime."

"About the case—or just to talk?" Her tone was teasing.

"Either. Maybe you'd like to give me your number?"

"I could make you work for it. I'll bet the FBI could find it out."

"I probably could, but I'd rather you gave it to me voluntarily."

She smiled and opened her purse. But she never had a chance to write down her number. The loud *crack!* of gunshots shattered the afternoon silence. Her screams rang in Graham's ears as he pushed her to the ground.

Chapter Three

Emma might have fantasized about Graham on top of her, but not like this. Gravel dug into her back, she couldn't breathe and her ears rang from the sound of gunshots. The smells of cordite and hot steel stung her nose, and she realized he had drawn a weapon and was firing. A car door slammed and then a revving engine and the squeal of tires signaled their assailant's escape.

Graham rolled off her, then took her hand and pulled her to her feet. "Are you all right?" he asked.

She brushed dirt from her skirt, and tried to nod, but she'd always been a lousy liar. Her legs felt like jelly and she was in danger of being sick to her stomach. "I think I need to sit down."

Ray and Lola emerged from the restaurant and crowded around them, followed by most of the waitstaff and half a dozen customers. "We called 911," Lola said. "What happened?"

"Someone shot at us." Graham put his arm around Emma. She leaned on him and let him lead her back inside. The reality of what had happened was beginning to sink in. They could have been killed—but why? "Can you bring us some brandy?" he asked.

Ray left and returned with a snifter of brandy. Graham held it to Emma's lips. "Drink this."

She did as he asked, then pushed the glass away, coughing, even as warmth flooded her. "I don't even like brandy," she gasped.

Graham handed her a handkerchief. It was clean, white linen and smelled of lemon and starch. She wiped her watery eyes, leaving a smear of black mascara on the pristine cloth. "If this is a typical date with you, I think I'm going to quit while I'm ahead."

She tried to return the handkerchief, but he waved it away. "You keep it. I promise you, this isn't typical."

"Did you see anything?" she asked. "The shooter, or their car?"

"A man dressed in black, wearing a ski mask and a watch cap. He drove a dark sedan, no license plate."

"I'm impressed you saw that much—I didn't see a thing."

"I make it a habit to notice things. The car was parked at the corner, waiting for us."

"So this was planned—not a random drive-by." She searched his face, hoping for some reassurance, but his expression was grave. Worried.

"I don't think so, no. Do you know anyone who might want you dead?"

The question brought another fit of coughing. "Don't sugarcoat it, okay?" she said when she could talk again. "What do you mean, does someone want me dead? What kind of a question is that?"

He patted her shoulder, his hand warm and reassuring. But these definitely weren't the circumstances in which she wanted to be bonding with a guy. "Can you think of any reason someone would want to shoot at you?" he asked.

The idea was as unsettling as the shots themselves. "No. I'm just a writer. And a nice person. I don't have enemies."

"Are you sure? Maybe you've written a story that's upset someone."

She shook her head. "No."

"What about Richard Prentice? What did he think of the profile you wrote about him?"

"He said he liked it—that I'd made him sympathetic. I mean, that's not what I set out to do, but that's how he took it."

"You said you've been a crime reporter. Has your reporting been responsible for putting any violent criminals away—people who might have vowed revenge?"

"I've reported on all kinds of crimes, but no one's ever threatened me, or even sent me angry letters." She knotted the handkerchief in her hand. "I thought that kind of thing only happened on television."

He squeezed her shoulder, and she fought the urge to lean into him and close her eyes. No, she had to be strong. "Tonight, when you've had time to think about it, I want you to make me a list of every story you've reported on that led—directly or indirectly—to the conviction of someone," he said. "We can run a check to see if any of them are out of prison. I'll work with the local police to determine if any of those people have been seen in the area."

"Shouldn't you leave this to the local police entirely? I thought your territory was the public lands."

He frowned. "It is. But when someone shoots at me, I take a personal interest."

"So maybe this isn't even about me." The

idea flooded her with relief. "Maybe the shooter was after you."

"That's possible."

"Maybe whoever shot Bobby decided to go after you."

"That's taking a big risk, considering we have no leads in that case."

"Maybe the person responsible doesn't know that."

He nodded. "Maybe not."

"Sir?" A uniformed police officer stepped into the alcove where they were sitting. "I'm Officer Evans, with the Montrose police."

"Captain Graham Ellison, FBI. And this is Emma Wade."

"I'll need a statement from each of you about what happened," Evans said.

"Of course."

A female officer joined them and led Emma away to question her about what had happened. Emma kept her answers brief; everything had happened so quickly she had few details to share. "What were you and Captain Ellison doing before the attack?" the officer asked.

"We were having dinner."

"You two are dating?"

The dinner had been like a first date. But not. "I'm a reporter and I was questioning him about a case he's working on."

"What case is that?"

"The Rangers found a downed plane in Curecanti Recreation Area today. The pilot had been shot."

The cop's eyes widened. "Murder?"

"It looks that way."

The officer shook her head. "When I joined the force, we might have had one violent death a year. In the past eighteen months we've had half a dozen. This task force doesn't seem to be doing much to slow things down."

Emma opened her mouth to defend Graham but stopped. Hadn't she had the same criticism of the task force? Knowing and liking Graham didn't change that opinion, did it?

"Did you see the shooter, or get a glimpse of the car?" the officer asked.

"No. Captain Ellison pushed me down as soon as we heard the first shot."

"And you have no idea who would want to shoot at you?"

"No. Maybe it's just one of those random things," she said. "Or a case of mistaken identity or something."

"Maybe so." The officer put away her pen and paper. "We'll do our best to find the person responsible. In the meantime, be careful."

The officer left and Graham rejoined her. "Let's go back to your place," he said.

She nodded. All she wanted was a hot bath and a cup of tea, and maybe a movie to distract her from all the horrors of today—first Bobby's death, then someone trying to kill her. It was too much.

When they reached her Jeep, Graham held out his hand. "I'll drive."

She started to argue—to tell him he was bossy and point out it was her car. "What about your Cruiser?" she asked.

"I can get it later."

Weariness won over stubbornness and she handed over the keys without another word.

Neither of them spoke on the drive to her house. She was still too numb for words, and he appeared lost in his own thoughts. But he swore as he pulled the Jeep to a stop in her driveway. She sat up straighter, heart pounding. "What is it? What's wrong?"

"You didn't leave your front door standing open when we left, did you?" he asked.

She stared at the entrance to her house, registering that the door was open. Then she was out of the car before she even realized what she was doing, running up the steps. "Janey!" she shouted. "Oh, Janey!"

JANEY THE CAT turned out to be fine, though she was clearly upset. They found her hiding under Emma's bed—a king-size affair with a puffy floral comforter and at least a dozen pillows. It looked feminine and soft and sexy—and it annoyed Graham that he could think these things while in the midst of a serious investigation.

"Is anything missing?" he asked as he followed Emma through the house, which looked undisturbed.

"I don't know. I don't think so. I was so worried about Janey I didn't even look." She cradled the cat to her chest and he felt a stab of envy. Yeah, he had it bad for this woman. *Focus*, he reminded himself.

"Then let's look together."

They checked the spare bedroom, living room and dining room. Everything was neat and orderly, nothing out of place. When they got to the kitchen she stopped. "My papers," she said.

"What papers?"

She pointed to the kitchen table, where a half-empty wineglass and a pen sat. "I was going over the notes I took today—at the press conference and at the crash site. They're gone."

She set down the cat and hurried back

into the living room and through a door to what turned out to be her office. "My laptop is gone," she said. She opened the accordion doors leading to a walk-in closet. "My files are gone, too."

"Which ones?"

"All of them." She pointed to the floor of the closet. "There was a rolling cart here, with two file drawers. It's gone."

"What was in the files?"

"Notes about articles I've written. Transcripts of interviews. Some photos."

"Everything?"

"The last couple of years' material. Anything older than that is in storage."

"You'll need to report this to the police," he said. "Then you can't stay here."

There he went, being bossy again. "Excuse me, but this is my home and I'll stay here if I want," she said.

"It's not safe." He turned away, as if that were the final declaration on the subject.

She grabbed his arm and pulled him back toward her. "Wait just a minute. We don't know if this is connected to the shooting or if the people who took my files mean me any harm."

"And we don't know that they don't. Do you want to take that chance?"

Of course she didn't. But she didn't want him thinking he could step in and rearrange her whole life for her. "I'm not leaving. I'll change the locks and I'll be careful, but I'm not leaving. Besides, where would I go?"

He pressed his lips together, as if debating his response. She crossed her arms over her chest and glared at him. "At least stay away for tonight," he said. "The police will want to come in and take photos, dust for prints. You can go to a hotel. While you're gone you can have someone in to change the locks."

He'd softened his tone—less bossy, more concerned. Her stomach knotted with indecision. She looked around and spotted Janey in the armchair where she liked to nap, busily grooming herself. "A hotel won't let me bring my cat and I won't leave her," she said. "Not when she's had such a terrifying day."

"Then stay with me. Janey can come, too." At her stunned look, he added, "I have a guest room. And a security system. No one will bother you."

"Fine." She was too tired—and yes, too scared—to argue anymore. "And thank you," she added.

She called the police and half an hour later found herself telling her story to an officer. While she dealt with the officers, Graham stepped out and made several calls. Every time she looked up she could see him out the window, pacing back and forth across her front lawn, phone to his ear. She had the feeling if she hadn't agreed to come with him tonight he would have insisted on staying and standing guard. She wavered between being touched by his kindness and concern, and annoyed at his overprotectiveness.

When the police told her she was free to go, she coaxed Janey into her carrier, packed an overnight bag and stowed everything in her Jeep. One of the officers had driven Graham back to the restaurant to retrieve his Cruiser, and she followed it out of town, toward the National Park to an upscale neighborhood of large lots and lovely homes.

Graham turned out to live in a cedar-sided cabin with large windows providing a view of open prairie and the distant lights of town. He helped her carry in her and Janey's things, stopping to punch a code into an alarm panel as soon as they entered. Then he led the way into a high-ceilinged great room. "Let me show you your room," he said.

The guest room was Spartan but adequate, with a queen-size bed, an armchair and a large bath across the hall. Without asking, he helped her set up Janey's litter box and bed, and filled the cat's water dish in the bathroom and brought it back. "Do you have any pets?" she asked.

"I had a cat at my last posting, but my schedule makes it tough on a pet, so I decided not to get another one after Buster died." He ran his hand along Janey's flank and she responded with a loud purr. "That's a pretty girl," he cooed, and Emma felt a flutter in her stomach, as if she were the one he was stroking.

He looked up at her. "How about if I fix us a drink?"

She nodded. "That sounds like a good idea."

She shut the door to the bedroom to give Janey time to settle in, then followed him into the living room. Though it was well into June, the night was cool, and he turned up the flame on a gas fireplace. "This is a gorgeous place," she said, accepting the glass of wine he offered.

"I can't claim any credit. A Realtor found it for me. Let's sit down." He motioned to the sofa.

She sat at one end of the leather couch; he settled at the other end, close enough that she could see the pulse beat at the base of his throat. She had a sudden memory of the feel of his body on hers, a heavy shield from danger.

"I'm sorry if I came across a little gruff earlier," he said. "I'm used to giving orders all day, and when I see a problem, my natural approach is to try to fix it."

"Except sometimes it's not your problem to fix." She sipped the wine and watched him over the rim of the glass. The apology had surprised her. She admired a man who could admit when he was wrong.

"Since I was with you when those shots were fired, my instinct has been to protect you. Call it sexist if you want, but that's how I feel."

"I've gotten used to looking after myself," she said. "But I appreciate everything you've done. If I'd been alone, I'm not sure I would have reacted so quickly to those shots." She shuddered, and set aside the glass.

"Hey, you did great." He set aside his own glass and slid over to her. "You kept your cool under pressure. That's one of the things I admire about you."

"Oh." Her eyes met his. "What else do you admire about me?"

"Would you think I was superficial if I said you have a beautiful body?" He caressed the side of her neck and brushed his lips across her cheek.

"Superficial can be good." She turned her

head and he covered her lips with his own. The kiss was hot and insistent. So much for holding back on their mutual attraction.

She slipped her arms around him and pressed against him, deepening the kiss. His body was big and powerful, and the need she sensed in him made her feel powerful, too. Maybe this was just what she needed, this physical distraction…

The strains of an Adele song jangled in the evening stillness. Graham raised his head and looked around. "My phone," she said, and reached for her purse.

Unknown number flashed on the screen, and she clicked the icon to answer, prepared to give a phone solicitor a piece of her mind. "Hello?"

"You need to stop now, before you get hurt," said a flat, accentless male voice.

"What are you talking about? Who is this?"

"If I'd wanted to kill you this evening, I would have," the voice said. "Next time, I won't miss."

The line went dead. Emma stared at the phone.

Graham took the device from her hand and set it aside. "I heard," he said. "Who has access to this number?"

"Lots of people," she said. "I mean, it's not

listed, but it's on my business cards. People at the *Post* have it. Friends. Business contacts." She rubbed her hands up and down her arms, suddenly cold. "Maybe this is just a prank. Somebody trying to unsettle me." She gave a shaky laugh, perilously close to hysterical tears. "And they're doing a good job of it."

Graham stood and pulled out his own phone. "I'll have someone trace the call, though I doubt it will do much good. It was probably made from a throwaway." His eyes met hers, and the hard look she found there frightened her all over again. "This isn't a joke, Emma," he said. "I think you're in real danger."

Chapter Four

Though Emma couldn't think of a safer place to be than Graham's spare bedroom, sleep still eluded her. Every time she closed her eyes, visions of what might have happened at the restaurant and the memory of that flat, menacing voice on the phone kept slumber at bay until the early hours.

Graham tapped on her door and awakened her a little after seven. "I wanted to let you sleep, but I have to get to the office," he said when she answered his knock. "I wasn't comfortable leaving you sleeping and alone."

His gaze drifted over her, and she was aware of her disheveled hair and the open robe over her nightgown. He wasn't leering or anything so crass, but she had the feeling if she'd suggested it, he wouldn't have hesitated to remove the crisp uniform he wore and join her back in bed.

She resolutely shoved aside the thought,

tempting as it was. As much as her body might have enjoyed the release, her mind wasn't ready for that kind of involvement with the intense captain. "Thanks for the coffee," she said, accepting the steaming cup he held out to her. "Do I have time for a shower?"

"Take all the time you need. I'll be in the kitchen."

By the time she'd finished the coffee, showered and dressed, she felt she had a better grip on her emotions. Janey curled up on a pillow and watched as Emma brushed out her hair and completed her makeup. Unlike her mistress, the cat had seemed perfectly content with their temporary quarters. "I'll agree the curmudgeonly captain has a certain charm," Emma said as she slipped on a pair of gold hoop earrings. "I just haven't decided if that makes up for the fact that he doesn't approve of what I do for a living." Though he'd probably never admit it, she was sure Graham still viewed journalists as his adversaries.

Janey followed her into the kitchen, where they found Graham serving up eggs and toast. "It's nothing fancy," he said, and set a plate in front of her.

"It looks great. Thanks."

He refilled her coffee, then set a bowl of water and another of food on the floor by the sink. "I opened up one of the cans of cat food you brought over."

Janey rubbed against his ankles, her purr audible across the room. "She never gets quite that enthusiastic when I feed her," Emma said, amused.

"I get along with most animals." He took the seat across from her.

"Just not most people," she said.

The corners of his mouth quirked up in acknowledgment of the gibe. He had nice lips, full and expressive. Her memory flashed to the kiss they'd shared last night, before the threatening phone call had destroyed the mood. What would have happened if the phone hadn't rung? Would she have spent the night in Graham's bed? And then what? They weren't exactly on the same side of things right now. Yes, she'd agreed to help him as much as she could, but she wasn't naive enough to believe he'd be even half as open with her. She'd have to dig and fight for information as much as ever. It didn't strike her as a good formula for a healthy relationship.

"Were you able to trace the call to my phone last night?" she asked.

He shook his head. "No luck. Anyone who watches television these days knows to use a cheap throwaway phone that can't be traced.

And if the caller really was the same person who shot at us yesterday afternoon, he's a professional."

"I still don't get why I'm a target all of a sudden," she said.

"What was in those notes that were stolen from your house?"

"Nothing that wasn't in the articles I wrote."

He took a bite of toast and crunched, a thoughtful look on his face. "You must take notes on some things that don't make it into the articles," he said after he'd swallowed.

"Oh sure—little details, background information—but nothing important."

"Were the notes you took during the weeks you spent with Richard Prentice in those files?"

"They were. Along with notes for a lot of stories. Everything I'd managed to pull together about Lauren Starling and her disappearance was in the file on the table. But why would they take everything?"

"Because they weren't certain what they were looking for? Or maybe they wanted to disguise their focus—take everything so it wouldn't be obvious what they were really interested in." He mopped egg from his plate with a triangle of toast and popped it into his mouth.

"It's not as if taking my notes would stop me from writing a story," she said. "I still have my memory, and my recorder—that was in my purse. I could even go back and interview people again."

"What are you working on right now?" he asked.

"I have to turn in a piece about your press conference yesterday."

He made a scoffing sound. "You couldn't have gotten much out of that."

"I'll have a few inches of copy, by the time I lay out the background behind the conference—Senator Mattheson's challenge and Richard Prentice's lawsuit."

"I can't see anything threatening in a story like that."

"I'm also providing background for a story on the plane crash and Bobby's murder, though because of my relationship to him, my editor is assigning another reporter to write the main article."

"Anything else?"

"I'm trying to find out everything I can about Lauren Starling and her disappearance."

"If it is a disappearance." He held up a hand to forestall the objection he must have known she'd have. "I'm not saying she isn't legitimately missing—only that we don't have proof of that yet. And she does have a history of erratic behavior."

"She didn't show up for work."

"At a job where she was rumored to be on her way out."

The sharp look he sent her told her he knew she'd underestimated him. "I guess you've been doing your homework," she said.

"I have. And everyone on the team has been on the lookout for any sign of Ms. Starling. Despite what you may think, we are taking this very seriously."

"That's good to know," she said. "And thank you for telling me. I know you didn't have to."

He nodded. "Back to the problem of whoever threatened you. Maybe there's something in your notes that you don't realize is important, but whoever took them does. Maybe something you noticed about Richard Prentice that he doesn't want someone to find out."

"Do you really think Richard Prentice is behind this, or is it just that the man has made himself such a thorn in your side?" she asked.

He stabbed at the last bite of egg on his plate. "I already told you, I don't have any proof that he's done anything wrong. I just have a feeling in my gut that he's up to something."

"Raul Meredes was operating near Prentice's estate, wasn't he?" The criminal with ties to a Mexican drug cartel had been killed while attempting to take a college student who was conducting research in the area hostage, but law enforcement officers at the scene swore they hadn't fired the shot that had ended his life. He'd been done in by a sniper, who fled as soon as Meredes was dead. The task force had linked Meredes to the deaths of several illegal immigrants in the park, who they suspected were part of a marijuana-growing operation and human-trafficking ring operating on public lands. If he'd lived to testify, he might have identified the person in charge of the operation.

"He would have had to cross Prentice's land to get to his operations," Graham said. "I don't believe for a minute that Prentice didn't know what was going on. The man has guards and cameras all over that place."

"Maybe he thought it wasn't his responsibility to report it," she said. "He'd say he shouldn't have to do law enforcement's job for them."

"He would say that, wouldn't he?" Graham's face twisted in an expression of disgust.

"Even if you're right and he's responsible for the crimes you're trying to control, why target me?" she asked. "I was with him for hours at a time for two weeks and he never showed the slightest hostility. And that was months ago. Why suddenly decide I'm a threat?"

"I don't know. Maybe it has something to do with the pilot who died."

"Bobby?" A dull pain centered in her chest at the memory of Bobby's lifeless body slumped in the seat of his plane. "We were just friends. We'd get together to talk, mainly. It wasn't anything serious."

"Maybe Prentice doesn't know that. He might have heard you two were dating and feared Bobby told you something he shouldn't have. Like what that plane was carrying, and who the cargo was intended for."

"What was the cargo?"

His expression grew wary. "We're still looking into that." He drank the last of his coffee. "If you're done with breakfast, we'd better go. I need to get to work."

"So do I." She carried her plate and cup to the sink. "I can wash up."

"Leave it. I have a woman who cleans for me. She'll take care of them. You're welcome to stay here as long as you like, though."

"No, I'll head back to my place. I'm sure the police have finished there by now."

He turned toward her, his big body filling the doorway, effectively blocking her in the kitchen. "I don't think it's a good idea for you to go there alone," he said. "Whoever attacked before could be waiting for you."

"He already took my notes and warned me off. He's not going to waste any more time with me." But she sounded more confident than she felt.

"Let me send someone with you. One of my men—"

"No! I do not need a babysitter." She told herself he was merely concerned, not being deliberately overbearing, and she softened her voice, trying to appear less angry at his suggestion. "I appreciate your concern, but I'll be fine," she said. "I promise I'll be careful."

"I don't like it."

"This isn't about what you like and don't like. I'm not your responsibility."

He opened his mouth as if to argue this point, too, but thought better of it. "Call me when you get to your place," he said. "Let me know you're okay." He hesitated, then added, "Please."

She wondered how much effort it took for him to add that last word. "I'll call you," she said. "I'm sure I'll be fine."

He stepped aside to let her pass and she retrieved her bag from the guest room. He helped her load it and the cat supplies into her

Jeep. "Thanks for taking me in last night," she said. "I think I would have been a lot more upset if I'd been alone when I got that call." Though she resisted his overprotectiveness, she had to admit his strong, calm presence last night had made her feel safe. She hadn't worried about anyone getting past him to get to her.

"I hope I'll see you again under better circumstances." He put a hand on her arm, his gaze focused on her mouth, as if debating the wisdom of another kiss.

She made the decision for him, leaning in to kiss him. The contact was brief, but intense, heat and awareness spreading through her. His grip tightened on her arm, but he didn't resist when she pulled away. "I'd better go," she said.

"Call me," he reminded.

"I will." And in the meantime, she'd try to figure out exactly what she felt for Captain Graham Ellison, and what she wanted to do about those feelings.

"SO THIS CRATE definitely contained a Hellfire missile?" Graham studied the debris they'd collected from the crash site, each piece tagged and cataloged, lined up on folding tables or set against the wall in a room in the trailer that had formerly been used to store supplies. The charred bits of wood and twisted scraps of metal told a story, though it was up to the task force to put that story together in the right order.

"According to the investigator the army sent over from Fort Carson, it did." Marco consulted a notepad. "They even know the serial number, a partial of which was stenciled on the box. If we find the missile, the numbers on the tail fin should match."

"Where did the missile come from?" Michael Dance, a tall, dark-haired lieutenant with the Border Patrol, asked. The newest member of the task force, he was also recently engaged to the woman who'd been instrumental in helping them find and target Raul Meredes. Abby was finishing up her masters in botany from the University of Colorado.

"Originally, from a shipment of Hellfires destined for Afghanistan," Marco said. "But a number of them disappeared along the way, probably to the black market in the Middle East and Africa."

"So, how did it end up here?" Carmen Redhorse, the sole female member of the task force, with the Colorado Bureau of Investigations, asked.

"Anyone with enough money can buy anything," Lance said.

"How much do you think one of these would sell for?" Michael nodded toward the busted crate.

Marco shrugged. "Half a mil? Maybe not that much, if you knew the right people."

Lance leaned against the door frame, arms crossed over his chest. "So who do we know around here with that kind of smack?" he asked.

"Being able to afford a missile doesn't mean Richard Prentice bought one," Carmen said.

"But the fact that the missile was on a plane flown by a man who was known to work for Prentice gives us reason to question him," Graham said. He turned to Lance. "What did you find out about Bobby Pace?"

Lance uncrossed his arms and stood up straight. "He keeps his plane in a hangar at Montrose Regional Airport. The Fixed Base Operations manager saw him there three days ago, checking out his plane, but Bobby said he didn't have a flight scheduled. I asked if he seemed nervous or anything, but the man I talked to—" he checked his notebook "—Eddie Silvada, said Bobby always seemed nervous lately. Jumpy. Silvada thought it was just because he'd been having financial problems. His kid has cancer and even with insurance, the treatments are expensive."

Graham nodded. This fit with what Emma had told him.

"Does he have other family in the area?" Carmen asked. "A wife?"

"Ex-wife," Lance said. "Susan Pace. They've been divorced a year and she says they don't talk much—just about the kid. She doesn't know what he was up to."

"A guy in that situation might be willing to fly an illegal cargo for a big payoff," Carmen said.

"When was the last time he filed a flight plan?" Graham asked.

"Last week," Lance said. "He flew an oil company photographer over a drilling site so he could get some aerial photos."

"When was the last time he flew for Prentice?" Michael asked.

"June 10. Almost two weeks ago. Before that he was flying him at least once a week, sometimes twice—to Denver and Salt Lake and other places where Prentice has business interests."

"Was Prentice using another pilot?" Carmen asked. "Did he and Pace have a falling out?"

"Or were they planning for Pace to pick up this missile and Prentice wanted to put some separation between them and provide himself with an alibi?" Graham asked.

"Do we know where Prentice was when Bobby was shot?" Lance asked.

"When was he shot?" Michael asked.

"The coroner thinks it was early Monday morning," Graham said. "Five or six hours before we found him."

"So what was Pace up to between Thursday and Monday?" Marco asked.

"And who was in that cockpit with him?" Michael asked. "Who shot him?"

"Someone could have met the plane at the crash site and shot him there," Carmen said. "The angle of the gunshot wound doesn't preclude that."

"We've got a couple of unidentified prints in the cockpit," Lance said. "Maybe a passenger."

Marco consulted his notes. "He was shot with a .38 caliber. A handgun, at close range."

"So someone was in the cockpit with him," Michael said. "They either flew in with him, or met him at the site and climbed in and shot him."

"The plane crashed on landing," Marco said. "The FAA and NTSB investigators are still sifting through the evidence, but something definitely went wrong in the air."

"Someone could have been following the plane on the ground," Lance said.

"Tough to do at night, with no roads," Michael said.

"Tough, but not impossible." Marco closed his notebook and stuffed it back into his pocket. "What next, boss?"

"I want you and Michael to go back to the airport," Graham said. "Talk to everyone at Fixed Base Operations—airport personnel, other pilots, anyone who might have seen Pace or talked to him. Find out if his plane was there on Friday or Saturday. Check the surrounding airports, too. Maybe he went to one of them to lay low for a few days."

"We'll get right on it." Michael said.

"Lance, you dig in to Pace's background. Look at his bank accounts, talk to his neighbors and his ex-wife, any friends."

"What do you want me to do?" Carmen asked.

"You're coming with me," Graham said. "It's time we paid another visit to Richard Prentice."

Chapter Five

Before she went home, Emma stopped at an office supply superstore and purchased a laptop to replace the one that had been stolen. She intended to get right to work, restoring her files and reconstructing as much of the missing notes as possible. But when she unlocked the front door and saw the state of her apartment, she formulated a plan B. She needed order and peace before she could focus on work.

She spent her first hour home cleaning up after the crime scene investigators. A lemon-scented spray vanquished fingerprint powder and smudges. If only it could wipe away this sense she had of being violated. Satisfied that order was restored, she made a cup of tea and set up the new laptop on the kitchen table. Though she had a home office, she preferred this bright, sunny room, with the teakettle close by and Janey stationed in her favorite perch on the windowsill overlooking the side yard, with its flower beds and bird feeder.

Thanks to online backup, she was able to restore most of her files within minutes. The articles she was working on, as well as those she'd written in the past, were available once more. Though she'd lost the handwritten notes she hadn't bothered to transcribe and some secondary sources, such as brochures and copies of reports, she had most of the stolen material here on her computer. If she read through it all, would she be able to figure out what the thief had been after?

She finished up the story of the press conference for the *Post*, along with information about Bobby and his death that the editor would incorporate into a story another reporter was already working on. Then she turned her attention to her notes on the missing woman, Lauren Starling.

Despite her best efforts, she didn't have much to go on in the case. The police in Denver had provided polite but unrevealing answers to her questions. The television station where Lauren worked had downplayed her disappearance, at first saying they weren't concerned then, when Emma had pressed, saying Miss Starling had a history of "health problems" that had forced her once before to take an extended leave of absence.

More digging had uncovered a three-week period the year before when Lauren had been absent from her job as one of the evening news anchors for Channel 9, but that hadn't turned up any further information, either. The woman wasn't married or in a serious relationship, and her only relative seemed to be a sister in Wisconsin, who hadn't returned Emma's calls.

"I don't see anything here that would lead anyone to warn me off," she said out loud to the cat. Talking out loud helped her organize her thoughts, and Janey pricked up her ears and tilted her head as if everything Emma said was fascinating. "So if it's not the story about Lauren Starling, what is it that's got this guy so riled?"

She ran her cursor over the lists of stories in her files and stopped when she came to her profile of Richard Prentice. She couldn't mesh the image of the intelligent, polite and sometimes charming host she'd written about with the criminal overlord Graham suspected him of being. Yes, Prentice held a grudge against the government, though she'd never been able to determine its source. He'd made a name for himself by fighting government regulation, government intervention and government restrictions, a stance that had made him a hero to many.

He was a ruthless businessman, someone who went after what he wanted with a single-mindedness few could match. But while some might justifiably charge that Prentice sometimes acted unethically, ethics weren't legislated in this country. What some people called immoral was simply good business tactics to others.

If he thought a story Emma was working on would get in his way, would Richard Prentice hire someone to threaten her, in order to make her stop? Maybe.

Would he hire a gunman to take a shot at her? She shook her head. Prentice was driven, but he wasn't insane.

But Graham didn't strike her as a man who jumped to conclusions. He'd been in law enforcement a long time. He'd seen crime in all its manifestations. If he suspected someone of wrongdoing, she had to seriously consider the suggestion.

Which meant that if Graham was right, and Prentice had been Raul Meredes's boss—and thus responsible for the death of half a dozen illegal immigrants—then he was a man who wouldn't blink at ordering someone to shoot at

a woman he wanted out of the way. Breaking into her apartment and taking a computer and some files paled in comparison to the crimes he'd already committed—or rather, had people commit at his behest. Prentice had the kind of money that insured he never had to get his hands dirty.

She read through the profile she'd written. Richard Prentice had been the middle child in a family with three children. He had an older brother and a younger sister, whom he saw rarely. He had an undistinguished educational career and had married young, only to divorce two years later, with no children. He started out in real estate, buying up old apartment buildings, renovating them and raising the rent.

From there, he'd expanded to other investments—everything from small factories to office parks and even amusement parks. He had a Midas touch when it came to making money in real estate and soon his millions multiplied to billions.

The public knew him best for the transactions that pitted him against the federal government. He had a genius for discovering private property near or surrounded by federal lands. He'd threaten to build an eyesore on the property, to destroy historical artifacts or to

construct a noxious business such as a paper mill or a commercial pig farm. He used the press to his advantage, willing to paint himself as the blackest villain in order to stir up public sentiment. Before long, the government would be agreeing to a trade—his precious tract for even more acreage elsewhere, or a large sum of money most grumbled was well over the actual market value of the property.

He'd used the same methods three times successfully. But when he purchased the large tract adjacent to the Black Canyon of the Gunnison National Park, he'd met a group of government officials who'd had enough. They refused to pay the price he demanded for the land, and quickly enacted enough restrictions to prevent any plans he had to exploit the property.

Emma suspected this was the source of much of his animosity toward local officials and The Ranger Brigade Task Force. He made a lot of speeches about the sanctity of private property rights and the oppression of parks that charged fees and were supported by taxpayer money. But Emma sensed the true cause of the undercurrent of rage he directed toward the Rangers was rooted in his frustration with being thwarted.

Which still didn't make him guilty of a crime.

"Was Bobby working for Prentice when he was killed in that plane?" she asked. Janey's answer was a yawn and a luxuriant stretch. "Who killed him, and why? And what was the mysterious cargo that Graham was so closed-mouthed about?"

Bobby had told her he liked working for Prentice. Or at least, he liked the generous paycheck the work generated. Robert Pace, Junior, who went by the nickname Robby, was on his second round of treatments for leukemia and the divorce decree stated that Bobby was responsible for all the medical bills not covered by insurance, which he also paid for.

Had Prentice—or someone—paid Bobby to smuggle drugs up from Mexico or South America? He wouldn't be the first pilot who'd make extra cash smuggling. Now that Colorado had legalized and regulated the production and sale of both recreational and medical marijuana, he might not even have seen what he was doing as so wrong. But bringing drugs—including marijuana—across state lines was still a serious federal crime.

Or maybe he'd been carrying cocaine or heroin or some other illegal substance. Graham knew, she was sure, and though she understood why he wouldn't want to blab the story to the press, it still stung that he didn't trust her.

She closed the file and rested her chin in her hands, brow furrowed in thought. Maybe whoever had killed Bobby thought she'd seen something at the crash site. Or maybe he thought if she kept digging, she'd uncover something he didn't want anyone to know.

She sat up straighter, her heart beating a little faster. "That has to be it, Janey." The man on the phone had warned her to stop what she was doing. What she did was investigate news stories—and the story of Bobby Pace's death was at the top of her list. She had a reputation as being good at getting to the truth of the matter, and in this case, Bobby's killer had a very good motivation for not wanting her to find him out.

She grabbed a notebook and began jotting down ideas and questions. Bobby was the key. She needed to find out what he'd been doing in that plane when it crashed—where he'd been, where he was headed, what he was carrying and who had hired him.

To find out, she'd start with the person who knew him best—the mother of his son and the woman who had been married to him for twelve years.

Susan Pace wore her bright pink hair in a pixie cut. Full-sleeve tattoos and multiple piercings in her ears, nose, eyebrows and lips gave the impression of a tough chick no one should mess with. But when Emma slid into the diner booth across from Susan and her son, Robby, she noticed the dark circles beneath the other woman's eyes, and the way she kept stroking and patting the boy, as if to reassure herself that he was still here. Susan might be tough, but she was also exhausted, frightened and hurting—a mother fighting for her child's life against an enemy that couldn't be intimidated by metal studs or tattoo ink.

"Thanks for agreeing to meet with me," Emma said, when they'd ordered coffee, and a milk shake for Robby. "I know you've got a lot on your plate right now."

"I was glad to get out of the house for a while." She smiled at the boy. "Robby's having a good day today, aren't you?"

Robby nodded. "I didn't throw up today," he said.

Emma's heart broke a little at that statement, said the way some boys might have announced that they'd hit a home run or gotten an A on a spelling test. Robby looked like his father, with Bobby's dark eyes, and the same dimple in his chin. She turned her attention back to Susan. "How are you doing?"

Susan shrugged. "Okay. The police were around, questioning me yesterday. About Bobby. I figure that's what you want to talk to me about, too."

Emma glanced at Robby. Susan sighed and reached into the pocket of her jeans and pulled out a handful of quarters. "Want to play video games, Robby?"

The boy's face lit up. "Yeah!"

"Here you go, then." She handed over the quarters and he scurried away. Both women watched him all the way across the room. He had to stand on tiptoe to reach the machine, but soon he was engrossed in the game.

"So, what did you want to ask me?" Susan asked.

"Someone broke into my house and stole all my notes. And I've received threatening phone calls. I think whoever killed Bobby is trying to stop me from writing about it."

Susan's eyes widened. "So what are you doing here now? If this person is a killer, why aren't you taking their advice?"

"Because I'm not that kind of person. I want to find out who they are—and why they killed Bobby."

Susan looked around nervously. "I don't

have any idea what Bobby was up to," she said. "We didn't talk about his work. What if this person who's been threatening you followed you here and sees you with me? I've got enough problems right now—I don't need some killer following me."

Emma took hold of the younger woman's wrist. "It's okay," she said. "Nobody is following me. We're just two friends having coffee."

Susan looked into her eyes, then nodded and pulled her hand away. She sipped her coffee. "Sorry," she said. "I'm just a little on edge. Bobby and I were divorced, but having him die like that—it really shook me up."

"How is Robby handling it?"

"I don't think he really understands what happened. I tried to explain to him about Daddy being in heaven now, but he knows Bobby flew planes. He'd been up with him a few times. So sometimes he talks about his dad flying to heaven—as if he's going to come back. The doctors were worried it might affect his treatment, but so far it hasn't."

"I know Bobby was paying the medical bills. Is that going to be a problem now? I could write an article for the paper..."

Susan shook her head. "You don't have to do that. With Bobby gone, Robby's eligible for Social Security and health insurance through the state. Is that twisted or what? Poor Bobby busted his butt to pay those bills, and now the government's picking up the tab."

"I'm glad you don't have to worry about that, at least," Emma said. "So, Bobby never talked about his work with you?"

"We had other things to talk about. More important things. He was a lousy husband, but he was a pretty good dad." She turned the teaspoon over and over on the table. "I know he'd been working a lot. And when I saw him a few days before…before he died, he told me he'd have enough money to pay most of the doctor bills soon. I figured that meant he had a new client, but I didn't ask about it. I didn't care how he got the money, as long as the bills were paid and Robby could get his treatments."

"Did you know he'd been flying for Richard Prentice?"

"The gazillionaire?" She nodded. "Yeah. He did a lot of work for him, and I guess that paid pretty well."

"Did he say where he and Prentice went?"

"I told you, I didn't care about that." She sat back and stared out the window, at the parking lot where the sun glinted on the rows of cars and traffic zipped by on the highway. "I know one time he flew Prentice and some other people all the way to South America. He was gone for a few days and had to miss one of Robby's chemo appointments." She glanced back at Emma. "He always tried to be there on chemo day."

"When was this—the South America trip?" Emma pulled out her reporter's notebook.

"I told the police this. It was maybe a month ago."

"Do you think he was working for Prentice on this last flight?"

"How would I know?" She sounded annoyed, but Emma was used to people being annoyed at her questions.

"Think. What, exactly, did he say about how he was getting the money to pay off the bills? Did he mention a man or a woman? A particular destination? Anything at all."

She furrowed her brow, and looked back over her shoulder to where Robby remained absorbed in the video game, his thumbs furiously flicking over the controls. "I think it was a woman," she said.

"You think the client was a woman?"

Susan nodded. "Before he told me about the money, he said he'd met this woman. I thought he was talking about a new girlfriend, but now I'm thinking maybe he didn't mean that at all."

"Bobby talked to you about the women he

dated?" Had he told Susan about the times he and Emma had gone out?

"No, he wasn't like that. I mean, I knew he dated. We were divorced, so he was a single guy with a plane—women like that. I liked that, once upon a time." Her expression hinted at a smile. "So I was a little annoyed when he started talking about this woman. I thought he was bragging or something. He said he'd try to get me an autograph—like she was someone famous or something. I thought he was just trying to be mean—letting me know what I was missing, or something. But it makes more sense if he was talking about a client."

"Did you tell the police any of this?"

"No. I just thought of it."

"What, exactly, did he say?"

"That he'd met a woman and they'd hit it off. They were supposed to meet again the next day and he'd try to get her autograph for me."

"Anything else?"

She made a face. "I wasn't very nice. I told him what he could do with that autograph. So then he told me he'd have the money for the bills soon."

"But you think this woman—this celebrity—was going to hire him to do a job?"

"Maybe. Or maybe it was just a date. But

Bobby never bragged about women that way. I even wondered after he left if he'd been drinking or something, but that wasn't like him, either. Still, having a sick kid can make you do all kinds of crazy things. I know."

"So he didn't say anything else about who this woman might be? I'm sorry I keep picking at this, but it's really important."

"I wish I could help you, but he didn't say anything else." She sat up straighter, a bright smile transforming her features. "Did you have a good time?"

Robby crawled into the booth beside her and laid his head against his shoulder. "I did, but I'm tired now. Can we go home?"

"We can." Susan hugged him close, then took her car keys from her pocket. "Thanks for the coffee," she said. "But we have to leave."

"Sure. Thanks for talking with me."

They left and the waitress refilled Emma's cup. She sat for a long time, sipping coffee and replaying the conversation over and over. She felt a little sick over what she'd discovered. She could think of only one female celebrity who could have been in Montrose in the days before Bobby's death.

But what was Bobby Pace doing with Lauren Starling?

Chapter Six

Imposing stone pillars and a massive iron gate marked the entrance to Richard Prentice's land, which he referred to as a ranch or an estate, depending on whom he was talking to. Though the road across the ranch had once been a public thoroughfare, Prentice had recently obtained a court order allowing him to close the road, hence the locked gate that confronted Graham and Carmen when they arrived.

He frowned up at the camera mounted on one of the pillars. "What now?" Carmen asked.

"He has guards, and I'm sure one of them is watching us."

"They could decide to ignore us."

"They could," he agreed. "But by now he's heard Bobby Pace is dead, and though he can deny a connection all he wants, there is one. If he doesn't at least pretend to cooperate with us, I can have him brought in for questioning."

"Someone's coming." She nodded toward an approaching cloud of dust.

The black Jeep skidded to a halt on the other side of the gate and two men in desert camo fatigues climbed out. The one on the passenger side carried an automatic rifle, its barrel pointed toward the ground. Graham recognized the driver from his last visit to the ranch, the day Raul Meredes died at the hands of an unknown sniper just as the task force was about to arrest him and bring him in for questioning. The shooting had occurred on national park land, within sight of the boundary to Prentice's holdings.

"We're here to see Mr. Prentice," Graham said, holding up the leather folder that contained his credentials.

"Any communication with law enforcement must go through Mr. Prentice's attorney," the young man said. "I can give you his contact information."

"I don't need it. I'm here to talk to Prentice."

The guard's expression remained impassive. "What is this in reference to?"

"One of his employees was caught red-handed with illegal goods."

"Who is the employee?"

"If Mr. Prentice wants you to know that, he can tell you."

The guard said nothing, but turned and walked back to the Jeep. A moment later, he and the man with the gun had driven away.

"What if he refuses to talk to us?" Carmen asked.

"Prentice likes to talk. I think he enjoys sparring with anyone in authority. But if he passes up this opportunity to play his favorite game, I can arrange with the lawyers to question him as a possible accessory to a crime."

"We don't have any proof that Bobby Pace was working for him at the time of the crash."

"We don't have any proof that he wasn't, either."

The Jeep returned ten minutes later. "He probably drove out of sight and made a phone call, then kept us waiting a few minutes longer for show," Graham said.

The guard didn't bother getting out of the Jeep this time. "You can follow us," he said.

He turned the Jeep around and the gate swung open behind him. Graham put the Cruiser in gear and followed him up the gravel road. Five minutes later, a massive three-story house built of gray stone loomed over them. With its flanking towers and expansive wings it resembled a castle, or a fortress.

"So this is what too much money will buy you," Carmen said.

"Can you have too much money?"

"I think so, yes."

Another camo-clad guard ushered them into the house, into a front room filled with bookshelves and comfortable chairs. Richard Prentice didn't keep them waiting. He strode into the room with the air of a much larger man, though he was well under six feet tall and rather delicate-looking. Still, he carried himself like a man who wielded great power. Having billions of dollars made up for a lot of shortcomings, Graham supposed.

"I'm a busy man, and I don't have time for small talk," he said by way of greeting. "What is this about an employee of mine smuggling something?"

"Bobby Pace flew for you," Graham said.

Prentice's eyes narrowed. "Pace was a private pilot I hired sometimes. Not lately, though."

"When was the last time he worked for you?"

"Two weeks ago? Maybe more."

"Have you spoken to him since then?"

"No."

"Are you sure?"

Graham could feel the anger radiating from the man, but Prentice kept his voice even, enunciating his words as if explaining a simple concept to a recalcitrant child. "I hired the man from time to time to do a job. We weren't friends."

No, Prentice would not be friends with someone like Bobby Pace. "Were you aware that Mr. Pace has a young son who is being treated for cancer?" Graham asked.

"I was not. What does this have to do with me? What does any of this have to do with me?"

"Where were you from Sunday night through Monday morning of this week?"

Prentice stiffened. "Why are you asking me these questions?"

"Answer the question please." Graham kept his voice pleasant.

"I was here."

"Can anyone verify that?"

"Everyone who works for me, I imagine. The guards at the gate, for a start."

"Do the guards know where you keep your drone?" Carmen asked.

Prentice didn't miss a beat. "What drone?"

She shrugged. "I heard a rumor that you'd purchased a drone."

"What would I want with a drone?"

"Some people use them for security," she said. "You can patrol a large area—like this ranch—with only a single operator and a camera attached to the drone."

"Interesting. Maybe I'll look into it."

"Maybe you should."

He turned back to Graham. "You've wasted enough of my time. You'd better go."

Graham thought about staying longer, if only to annoy the man. But Prentice wasn't the only busy person in the room. "We'll be in touch," he said, and led the way back to the Cruiser.

"Why do I feel I've just poked a stick in a very big fire ant bed?" Carmen asked as they pulled away from the house. "We annoyed him and didn't learn anything useful."

"I wouldn't say that." Graham checked his rearview mirror. The Jeep with the two guards had fallen in behind them, escorting them to the main road.

"What do you mean?" Carmen asked.

"He wanted to know why I was questioning him about an employee smuggling something. But I never used the word *smuggling*. I said the employee had been caught with illegal goods."

"Do you think it means anything?" she asked.

"He knows more than he wants us to believe. I think he's hiding something."

"Maybe that drone," she said.

"Or a Hellfire missile. Or maybe something even bigger. Whatever it is, I'm going to find it."

"IF YOU LIKE, MA'AM, I can tell the captain you were here and ask him to call you." The Ranger, a young man with closely cropped blond hair and a nametag that read Sgt. Carpenter, hovered near her as she walked around the room in the trailer that served as Ranger headquarters. He reminded her of an Australian shepherd, ready to herd her away from anything that was off-limits. In fact, he looked as if he wanted to herd her right out of the office.

"I don't mind waiting for Graham to return." She took a seat in one of the gray metal folding chairs arranged around an equally utilitarian folding table and crossed her legs, her skirt riding up—just a little—on her thigh. Along with the gray pencil skirt she wore a scoop-necked knit blouse and four-inch red high heels. She might be here on serious business, but she wanted to make sure she held Graham's attention. Sergeant Carpenter looked even more nervous.

"He might not be back for a while," he said.

"I've got time." She smiled at him, the picture of the calm, collected journalist prepared to wait all night, if necessary. Though really, she felt ready to jump out of her skin. She needed to talk to Graham—in person. The things she'd learned from Susan Pace could change his whole investigation. Graham thought Bobby's murder wasn't connected to Lauren's disappearance, but now she was sure they were related. Maybe this was the break they needed to find the missing woman. Maybe it wasn't too late to save her.

"I guess that's all right, if it's what you want," Carpenter said, though he looked doubtful. He probably realized he didn't have a choice but to accept her presence. He'd have a tough time dragging her out of there by himself. He took up a position across the room, leaning against the wall, arms folded, eyes fixed on her.

"I don't mean to keep you, Sergeant," she said. She took out her phone and pretended to read something on the screen. "You can return to whatever you were doing. I'll entertain myself."

"I don't think the captain would like it if I left you here alone," he said.

Which she translated to mean he wasn't about to give her the opportunity to snoop around. That did sound like Graham. He might open his home to a woman in distress, but he wasn't going to trust a reporter.

For the next twenty minutes, she scrolled through messages on her phone while Sergeant Carpenter held up the wall and scowled at her. She debated telephoning Graham and telling him she was waiting for him, but she didn't want to give him the opportunity to put her off. If she was sitting here in his office when he returned, he'd have to listen to her.

The pop of gravel beneath the tires of a vehicle made her sit up straighter. Carpenter peered between the blinds on the window beside him. "He's here," he announced.

Emma was on her feet and halfway to the door when Graham strode in. She caught her breath at the sight of him. How had she forgotten how impressive he was? He exuded strength and command...and sex appeal. The speech she'd rehearsed went right out of her head as she remembered the kiss they'd shared last night.

"Emma! What are you doing here? Is everything all right?" He closed the gap between them in two strides and grasped her shoulders. "Has something else happened? Another threat?"

His obvious concern for her made her a little weak in the knees, but she rallied and shook her head. "Nothing like that. I'm fine." Gently, she stepped out of his grasp. "But I've learned something important. Something about Bobby."

"Come into my office." One hand at her back, he guided her into a small room to the side and closed the door behind them. He motioned her to another folding chair, and took a seat behind his desk. "What is it? Did you remember something about Pace?"

"I talked with his ex-wife this afternoon. Susan."

A deep V formed between his eyebrows. "We've already interviewed her."

"I'm sure you did, but sometimes another woman—someone who isn't in law enforcement—can learn things you can't."

"What did you learn?"

"She talked to Bobby a few days before he died. He mentioned a woman—a celebrity—he was seeing, and that he'd have the money soon to pay off his son's medical bills. I think he was talking about Lauren Starling. I think she hired Bobby to fly for her."

"Susan Pace said that Bobby was working for Lauren Starling?"

"She didn't say the name—only that he talked about a woman he'd met, that she was famous and he'd try to get Susan an autograph."

She expected him to be excited about this breakthrough, or to at least show some interest. Instead, he blew out a breath, impatient. "Emma, he was probably talking about you," he said. "You two were dating, and you're a well-known journalist."

Under less serious circumstances, she would have laughed. "Graham, I'm not famous!" she said. "Bobby certainly didn't think of me that way."

"Your byline is in the paper all the time. People know you."

"That's not celebrity. Not like Lauren Starling, whose gorgeous face was on television every night."

He pressed his lips into a thin line, as if he was trying not to say everything he thought. "Susan Pace never mentioned any of this to my team when they interviewed her," he said. "She said she had no idea who Bobby was working for or what he was doing."

"And that's true." Emma sat on the edge of the chair and leaned toward him. "She didn't think this woman was important. But when I pressed her, she remembered her."

"I still think he was talking about you."

"And I'm sure he wasn't." It was her turn to be impatient with him. "Journalists aren't celebrities. No one wants our autograph. Besides, Susan told me Bobby didn't brag about the women he dated. So this wasn't a date—it was a client. It had to be Lauren. There's a connection you need to check out."

"Nothing we've found indicates any link between Bobby Pace and Lauren Starling," he said. "No one we've talked to has reported seeing them together. None of the evidence from the crash points to her."

"But Susan—"

"Doesn't know the name of this woman and can't even say whether her husband was talking about a client or a date." He shook his head. "I'm sorry, Emma, but at this point, it doesn't help."

"So you don't believe there's any connection between Lauren and Bobby?"

"It's not about what I believe. What matters is what I can prove. Investigations aren't built on hunches, they're based on evidence."

"So you're not going to look into this further?"

"There's nothing to look into." The edge in his voice was sharp enough to cut flesh.

She stood, swallowing hard to keep from telling him exactly what she thought of him and his disregard for what she saw as vital information. "If you were willing to unbend enough to at least consider the possibility that Lauren is involved in this case, you might find your precious evidence."

He sighed, a long-suffering, patronizing sigh that made her want to scratch his eyes out. "Emma," he began.

"Don't say it," she said between clenched teeth.

"Don't say what?"

"Whatever patronizing, dismissive thing you were going to say. I already get the message. I won't bother you anymore."

"Emma! Wait!" He rose, but she turned and headed toward the door. She had to get out of there before he tried to talk her into staying. She couldn't let her physical attraction to the man overcome her loathing for someone who wouldn't listen to her.

Chapter Seven

Graham stared after Emma, seething. Of all the unreasonable, pigheaded, unjustified shortsighted...

Lance tapped on the door frame. "Everything okay?" he asked.

"Fine." Graham bit off the word.

"Ms. Wade didn't look too happy," Lance said.

Graham grunted.

"Looks like she has a temper to match her hair." Lance lowered himself into the chair Emma had just vacated. "What did she want?"

"She wanted me to investigate the connection between Bobby Pace and Lauren Starling. Except there is no connection—no evidence that points to one except Emma's obsession with this Starling woman."

"She thinks the two of them know each other?"

"She's leaping to conclusions." Graham

began opening and shutting desk drawers. If he still smoked, this would be the time for a cigarette, but he'd given up the habit five years ago. "Pace's ex said he mentioned seeing a woman who was a celebrity. On the basis of that, Emma has developed a whole theory that Starling hired Pace to fly her somewhere."

"It does sound a little thin. Want me to check it out?"

"There's nothing to check. We already interviewed everyone connected with Pace, and no one mentioned a woman—celebrity or otherwise."

"So we talk to them again. Sometimes people remember things better when you ask a second time."

"No. Don't waste your time. I'm more concerned with Pace's connection to Richard Prentice. Any luck there?"

"I've got copies of the flight plans he filed with the local airport. Lots of trips with Prentice, once a week or so for about four months, then nothing. I can't find where Prentice was flying with anyone else at that time, but he may have been using another airport."

Graham massaged the bridge of his nose, grimacing.

"Headache?" Lance asked.

"This day's been nothing but one big headache." He shoved up from his desk. "I'm calling it a day. It's after five, anyway, and I'm not getting anything accomplished."

"See you tomorrow," Lance said. "Maybe we'll catch a break."

"Maybe."

Graham drove home in a dark mood. When he walked in the door, the first thing he smelled was Emma's perfume. Maybe he was imagining it—after all, the cleaning lady had been in that day. The place ought to smell like the lemon-scented stuff she used on the counters and floors. Instead, the soft aroma of roses surrounded him.

He walked to the kitchen and pulled a beer from the refrigerator. When he opened the trash can to drop in the bottle cap, he spied the cat food can where he'd fed her cat, Janey. Maybe he should get another cat. It would beat coming home to an empty house.

Restless, he wandered the house. He should change into workout gear and go for a run. That would clear his head. But on the way to his bedroom, he stopped outside the open door to the guest room. The cleaner had stripped the sheets, but he could imagine Emma standing before the mirror on the dresser, brushing out those red-gold locks.

With a groan, he turned away.

Five miles later he was sweating and tired, sure that a shower and a good night's sleep would set him right. But sleep eluded him. He spent the dark hours replaying their conversation, wondering what he could have said or done to make things come out differently.

He rose early the next morning and, after strong coffee and a bagel, headed for the airport. The Montrose Regional Airport was a small airfield that served a mix of commercial and private planes. Fixed Base Operations, headquartered in a low square building among the private hangars, was a buzz of activity in the early morning. Graham found a trio of pilots gathered in the lounge, drinking coffee, consulting charts, waiting for their turn to take off. When he walked in, several took in his uniform and soon they all fell silent, watching him.

"Did any of you know Bobby Pace?" he asked.

They exchanged glances. One of them, a younger man with sunglasses pushed to the top of his head and a red-and-blue plaid shirt open over a stained white T-shirt, said. "A lot of us knew Bobby. Shame about what happened to him."

"I'm trying to find whoever shot him," Graham said. "But I'm running into a wall. No one seems to know who he was flying for when he was killed."

"Can't help you there," the young man said. "Last time I saw Bobby was maybe a week ago. He wasn't flying that day, just hanging around, shooting the breeze, hoping somebody might walk in and want his services."

"He was always looking for work." Another man, thin and hunched with lines carving a face like a walnut, spoke up. "We knew he had a sick kid, so we tried to help him."

"Do people wander in here looking for a pilot that often?" Graham asked.

"Now and then," the old guy said. "Tourists, or folks in a hurry to get somewhere. If they got the money and it ain't illegal, I'll fly 'em."

"Do people sometimes want illegal things?" Graham asked.

The old man made a snorting sound. "I stay away from any of that."

"What about Bobby? Did he stay away from the illegal stuff?"

Again, they traded glances. "Bobby was desperate," the young man said. "He might look the other way if the money was right."

"What kinds of things did he do?" Graham asked.

"I don't like to speak ill of the dead." The young guy looked nervous.

"Nothing big." The older guy took up the conversation. "Maybe he'd file a flight plan for a certain route and deviate from the route a little to drop off a passenger who didn't want everybody to know where he was going. Little things like that."

"We haven't been able to find the flight plan he filed for the day he was killed," Graham said.

"He probably didn't file one," the old man said.

"I don't think he flew from here that day," the younger man said.

"Why do you say that?" Graham said.

"I don't remember seeing his plane for a few days before that. I thought he was out of town."

"Where did he keep his plane?" Graham asked.

"He parked it out past the northwest runway. I keep my plane out there, too."

"Not in a hangar?"

"Hangar space is more expensive," the old man said.

"Did any of you ever see him out here with a woman?" Graham asked. "Did he have any women clients?"

"He had a female student for a while." The third man, short, balding and middle-aged, spoke for the first time. "Sheila or Sherry or something like that. She was a student over at Western State. But that was a while ago. Maybe six months back."

"What happened to her?" Graham asked.

"She moved, I think," the young guy said. "Anyway, she stopped coming around."

"No other women clients you know about?" Graham asked.

All three shook their heads.

"What about girlfriends? Did he ever bring them out here?"

"I never saw him with anybody," the old guy said.

"I got the impression he didn't date much," the young guy said. "I think he still carried a torch for his wife."

"He might have had a woman over by his plane a few days ago," the middle-aged guy said. "But I don't know if it was a girlfriend or a client. He and whoever this was were in his plane, and they were arguing about something. I thought the other person's voice was kind of high-pitched, but I couldn't see who it was. All I heard was raised voices, so I steered clear."

"When was this?"

The man squinted, as if examining an imaginary calendar. "Monday a week ago, I think."

"Did either of you hear or see anything?" Graham asked the other two.

They shook their heads. "Sorry we can't help you," the younger man said. "I hope you find who killed him. That's kind of scary, you know?"

They began to move away. Graham thought about pressing, but he thought it unlikely he'd get any more information out of them. He spent the rest of the morning talking to the FBO manager, a secretary and a mechanic who looked after the planes. All of them were sorry Bobby was gone, but they didn't know who he was working for, and none of them had seen him with a woman.

So, was Emma right? Had Bobby had a mysterious—famous—female client in the week before he died? Or was Graham right and the woman was Emma herself? She'd said she and Bobby were just good friends, but did the relationship go deeper? Was she hiding something from him? Had they argued and she was reluctant to admit it, either because it implicated her somehow, or simply because she didn't want to speak ill of the dead?

By the time he arrived at Ranger headquarters in the park, he had decided he'd have to speak to Emma again, to question her more about her relationship with Bobby Pace. He wasn't looking forward to what he was sure would be a tense conversation, but it had to be done, and he wasn't going to put it off on another member of the team. He wanted to hear the truth himself from Emma's lips. She was already angry with him, so what did it matter if he upset her more? Though the thought twisted his stomach into knots.

Carmen met him at the door to the office, her normally serene face a mask of worry. "We've been trying to reach you all morning," she said.

"I had my phone off." He hadn't wanted to be interrupted while he was at the airport, then in his turmoil over Emma, he'd forgotten to turn it back on. He switched it on now, and in a few moments, message alerts began scrolling across the screen. "What's up?" he asked.

"In your office. There're some papers there you need to see."

"I'm not going to like whatever it is, am I?" he asked.

She shook her head. "Sorry. No."

The thick, legal-size stack of papers in the center of the blotter on his desk didn't hold the promise of anything good. Carmen and Randall Knightbridge followed him into the office and watched as he picked up the sheaf of documents and scanned them.

"Richard Prentice is *suing* us?" The words came out as a roar. He felt like punching something, but of course, that wasn't how a commander behaved, so he settled for dropping the papers back onto the desk and began to pace. "He says we're harassing him—am I reading that right?"

"That's what I got out of all that legalese," Randall said. "He accuses us of trespassing on his property, harassing his employees and him, and making false accusations against him."

"We've had legitimate reasons to question him every time we've done so," Graham said.

"He thinks we're picking on him because he's rich," Carmen said.

Graham pulled out his phone.

"Who are you calling?" Randall asked.

"Not Prentice. No sense adding fuel to the fire." A moment later, Graham connected with a federal attorney in Denver. Yes, he had received copies of the lawsuit. No, he didn't think Prentice had grounds for legal action, but they needed to tread carefully. After ten minutes, Graham disconnected the call, feeling no calmer, but somewhat resigned.

"Well?" Randall asked.

"That was our lawyer. He says to back off Prentice for now and see how this plays out." He sank into his chair and checked the clock. Only eleven. He still had a long day to get through. "Let's get back to work." He needed to type up the notes from the morning's interviews, and come up with a list of questions to ask Emma. Emma again—why couldn't he get her out of his thoughts for even half an hour? The woman was seriously messing with his head. He rubbed the bridge of his nose and tried to remember where in his desk he'd stashed a bottle of aspirin.

When he looked up, Carmen and Randall were still standing there, eyeing him nervously.

"What is it?" he asked. He looked around. "And where is everyone else? What's going on?"

"There's something else you need to see." Carmen gestured toward the desk. "Under the legal papers."

"Where is everyone else?" Graham asked again.

"They went out." Randall looked as if he didn't feel very well.

Understanding dawned. "You two got the short straw," he said. "You had to stay here with me and deliver the bad news."

"Something like that," Carmen said.

He sighed. Whatever it was, it couldn't be much worse than the lawsuit. He set aside the legal documents and looked down at this morning's edition of the *Denver Post*. The headline was about the latest fracas in the Middle East. "What am I supposed to be so upset about?" he asked.

"Turn the paper over," Carmen said. "Below the fold."

He flipped the paper and read the bold lettering splashed across the bottom third of the paper. At first, the words didn't quite register, then his vision dimmed, his brain fogging with disbelief and rage. He blinked and read the words again. *Link Between Starling Disappearance and Pilot's Murder Goes Unexplored By Law Enforcement.*

He didn't have to check the byline to know who had written the story, but he did, anyway. *By Emma Wade, Post Western Slope Bureau.*

Chapter Eight

Emma spent the morning in her home office waiting for Graham. She didn't know whether he'd call to chew her out, or show up in person, but she was sure he'd have some response to the article in this morning's paper. She hadn't said anything in there that wasn't true; she didn't claim to have proof, only a suspicion, and had spent much of the piece pleading for the mysterious female client to come forth, if it was someone other than Lauren Starling.

But she hadn't pulled any punches, either. She'd found someone from the television station to say that they thought local authorities should be investigating every possible sighting of Ms. Starling, while someone else told how people often asked Lauren for her autograph. "She was—is—glamorous and beautiful and we all thought of her as a celebrity," the coworker said.

In case Graham showed up in person,

Emma dressed carefully, in a formfitting gray pencil skirt, red V-neck sweater and the confidence-inspiring red heels. Maybe he hated her now, but it wouldn't hurt to remind him what he was missing by making her his enemy.

By eleven o'clock she wondered if he'd decided to ignore her. She hadn't figured the captain would play things cool, but maybe she'd read him wrong. Maybe goading him this way hadn't been the best approach to getting him moving.

When the doorbell rang at eleven thirty, she jumped, heart pounding. The sight of Graham's big profile—and scowling face—made her debate retreating to the bedroom and pretending not to be home. But she wasn't a coward. She took a deep, steadying breath, and opened the door. "What took you so long?" she said, before he could speak.

He moved forward, giving her no choice but to back up or be run over. "You did this deliberately," he said, his voice low and ragged, eyes burning with rage.

"You wouldn't even listen to me yesterday," she said. "You treated me like some crackpot off the street with a story I'd made up out of whole cloth. This was the only way I knew to get you to pay attention."

"You embarrassed me and my team in front

of the whole state," he said. "You couldn't trust me to do my job."

"You weren't doing your job." Her voice broke on the last word, and she cursed the lapse. She needed to stay cool and detached, to not let him get to her.

"I spent the morning at the airport, talking to people who knew Bobby Pace," he said. "Trying to find this mysterious woman. I know how to do my job."

She swallowed. *Uh-oh.* "I… The way you acted yesterday, I didn't think you took me seriously."

"Just because others before me didn't listen to you, doesn't mean I'd make the same mistake." He took another step toward her, forcing her to move farther into the house. He was breathing hard, his face flushed, hands clenched at his sides. She ought to be terrified, but he didn't frighten her. A sense of anticipation, of wondering what would happen next, made her a little unsteady on her feet, but determined to hold her ground.

"I'm sorry," she whispered. "I never meant to hurt you."

He moved closer, crowding her against the wall. In her heels, they were almost the same height; she looked him right in the eye and what she saw there made her insides feel molten. Graham Ellison wanted her, as fiercely as she wanted him. She moistened her suddenly dry lips, his eyes tracking the movement of her tongue.

"You're driving me crazy, did you know that?" he said, his voice almost a growl, the low cadence vibrating through her, like a physical touch.

"There's definitely a...connection," she said, more breathily than she would have liked. She'd always prided herself on being able to hide her emotions from other people, a talent that came in handy as an investigative reporter. But with Graham she felt defenseless, stripped bare.

"Why you?" he asked. "Why have I got it so bad for a woman who will bring me nothing but trouble?"

"I'm not your enemy," she said. "We both want a murderer brought to justice and a missing woman to be found safe."

"But I've got the law on my side. You're just a loose cannon." His gaze raked her, settling on the hint of cleavage at the neckline of her top.

She pressed her shoulders against the wall and tilted her pelvis forward, brushing against him. "I think the wildness in me is part of the attraction," she said. "You wouldn't want a tame pet you could control."

In answer he put his hands on her hips and dragged her to him. His mouth crushed against her, fierce and demanding. She arched against him, a thrill racing through her at his strength and power. She slid her arms around his neck and slanted her lips more firmly against his, deepening the kiss. His heart hammered against her—or maybe that was the driving pulse in her own arteries.

Still holding her against him, he abandoned her mouth and dipped his head to trace his tongue along the curve of her cleavage. "What are we going to do about these feelings we have for each other?" she asked.

"I want to take you to bed and make love to you until we're both too exhausted to think about it." He nuzzled at the side of her neck.

"That...that sounds like a good plan."

He slid down the zipper at the side of her skirt and began pushing it down her hips. She grabbed his wrist. "Let's go into the bedroom, where we'll both be more comfortable."

Holding the skirt with one hand and him with the other, she led him into her room. She released him long enough to scoop Janey off the pillow and toss her gently in the hallway. She shut the door and faced him again. His eyes still burned with desire, but some of the earlier caution had returned. "Are you sure this is a good idea?" he asked.

"I think if we don't do this, neither one of us is going to think about anything else when we're together."

He nodded. "So, you're just trying to get me out of your system."

"I don't think shaking you is going to be as easy as all that." She moved closer and undid the top button of his uniform shirt. "It will probably take a lot of effort and practice. Months." She kissed the triangle of chest now exposed. "Even years."

She worked her way down his chest, unbuttoning and kissing, until she reached his navel, and the barrier of his utility belt. "I'll take it from here," he said, and pulled her up to kiss her once more, as his hands fumbled with the belt and trousers.

She broke the kiss and pushed away. "Where are you going?" he asked.

"Not far." She slipped into the bathroom and returned a moment later with a condom, which she placed on the nightstand. "When you're ready," she said.

"Oh, I'm ready all right." He pushed down his pants and she saw how ready.

"Captain, I'd say you were armed and

dangerous." She finished unzipping the skirt and let it drop, then pulled off her blouse, so that she stood in front of him in her underwear and the red heels.

He grinned and reached for her. "Better than my best fantasies," he said.

She wasn't the flat-stomached, thin-thighed, cellulite-free version of a woman popular with magazines and television shows, but the look in Graham's eyes—and the eager movements of his stroking hands and caressing lips—told her he liked what he saw just fine. She'd vowed years ago to stop apologizing for her body and to focus on enjoying it. Graham made that vow easy to keep. In his arms she felt as sexy and womanly as she ever had.

When they were both naked, they lay back on her bed. "When I saw that article in the *Post*, I was so angry," he said.

"So I gathered." She suppressed a giggle.

"What's so funny?" he asked.

"When I opened my door and saw you standing there, you looked like a bull ready to charge." She flattened her palm against his chest and pushed him back against the mattress. "You were magnificent. I wanted to tear your clothes off right there in the doorway."

"Oh, you did?" He smoothed his hand along the curve of her hip. "Part of me was glad about the article, too. Because it gave me an excuse to come over and see you." He kissed her, long and deep, until she was dizzy and out of breath. He cupped his hand between her thighs and she moaned, a fresh wave of need and longing engulfing her.

He rolled her over, until she was pinned beneath him, then he lavished attention on first one breast, then the other, all while his fingers played between her legs.

She writhed beneath him, incoherent with desire. She could feel his erection pressed against her thigh, hot and heavy. He planted his knee firmly between her thighs. "You are a wild one, aren't you?"

She stared up at him, unspeaking, waiting to see what he would do. He took the condom from the nightstand and ripped open the packet, then slowly rolled it on. "Ready?" he asked.

"I've been ready." She wrapped her hand around him, guiding him toward her. "Stop wasting time."

He laughed and entered her, filling her, his laughter vibrating through her. He was always such a serious man—that he could laugh while making love to her made her feel a sudden tenderness for him, even as the passion between them began to build once more. She tightened around him, gratified by the glazed look that came into his eyes, and the long sigh that escaped from his lips. They moved together, meeting each other stroke for stroke, and she wanted to shout for the joy of it.

She did shout when her climax overtook her, and wrapped her legs around him, holding him to her as he found his own release. She reveled in the strength of his muscles moving against her, and the hard pounding of their hearts, almost in unison. She continued to hold him as he gently slid from her and lay beside her. Eyes closed, he breathed heavily, his face pressed against her neck.

"That was pretty incredible," he said after a while.

"Mmm." She closed her eyes, the afterglow of great sex humming through her. "It was." And Graham Ellison was pretty incredible, too. Handsome, strong, sexy—also stubborn, opinionated and too harsh in his judgment of the press. But she wasn't going to think about that right now. She wasn't going to think about anything but how right it felt to be with him in this moment, however fleeting the sensation might last.

GRAHAM CRADLED EMMA'S head on his shoulder, eyes closed, half dozing. He couldn't believe his luck, ending up with this gorgeous, sexy woman. And she was right—he wouldn't be as happy with a woman with no spirit. He liked that she stood up to him, no matter how much she aggravated him at times.

He leaned over and buried his nose in her hair, inhaling the sweet scent of roses and vanilla.

And smoke.

The acrid stench of burning wood and wiring brought him fully awake. He shook Emma. "Get up! The house is on fire!" Smoke curled around the bedroom door, a gray ghost of horror.

"Wh-what?" She sat up, hair tousled, clutching at the sheets.

"The house is on fire. We have to get out of here." He found his pants on the floor by the bed and began putting them on.

Emma stumbled out of bed and pulled on her robe. She looked around, frantic.

"Shoes," Graham instructed, shoving his sockless feet into his boots. He moved to the door and pressed his palm against it. It wasn't hot. A peek into the hallway showed the fire hadn't yet reached this far, though the glow of orange flame and the crackle of collapsing wood told him the front room was ablaze.

He returned to Emma and grabbed her

hand. “Come on,” he said. “We’ve got to get out of here.”

Wordlessly, she followed him to the kitchen. Though smoke filled the room, it was flame-free and he was able to lead them to the back door. With his free hand, he felt in his pocket for his phone. As soon as they were both in the clear, he’d call for help. He jerked open the door, cool air bathing them like a soothing balm.

They were almost down the back steps when Emma jerked from his grasp. “Janey!” she cried. “I have to get Janey!” She turned and raced back into the house, back into the smoke and flames.

Chapter Nine

"Emma, no!" Graham lunged for her, but she slipped from his grasp. He raced after her, but got only as far as the kitchen door before smoke and heat forced him back. His eyes stung and his lungs burned as he tried to see through the dense black smoke. "Emma!" he shouted, but could barely hear his own voice over the pop and crackle of the flames.

Had she headed back to the bedroom, or to the front room? He had no way of knowing, and both rooms appeared to be a wall of smoke and flame. Reluctantly, he retreated to the back door, driven back by the ferocity of the blaze. As he stumbled down the steps, sirens wailed in the distance; a neighbor or passerby must have seen the fire and called it in.

Someone grasped him by his shoulders: a balding man in glasses and wide, frightened eyes. "Are you all right?" the man asked.

Graham nodded and coughed. “There’s a woman still inside.”

“Emma?”

“Yes.” Through eyes still stinging from smoke, he stared at the burning house, now fully engulfed in flames.

The man looked even more frightened. “I don’t think anyone’s coming out of there,” he said.

The idea enraged Graham. Why had he let her go? Why hadn’t he held on and insisted she come with him? He scanned the back of the house and found the bedroom window. If she’d gone that way, maybe he could reach her.

He shoved to his feet, jogged to the window and tried to pull it up, but it refused to yield. He looked around and spotted a large ceramic flowerpot. He jerked up the heavy pot and hurled it through the window, then stuck his head inside. “Emma!”

“Graham?” Her voice was faint and choked.

“Emma! I’m at the window.”

A moment later, she emerged from the blackness, and thrust a bundle into his hands. “Take Janey,” she commanded.

He took the cat, which was wrapped in a towel, and tucked it into the crook of one arm, then reached for Emma with the other. She tumbled out the window, onto the ground beside him, her face streaked with smoke, her robe scorched from cinders.

He half carried her, half dragged her farther from the burning building. “If I weren’t so happy to see you, I’d wring your neck,” he said, kneeling beside her and cradling her face in his hand.

“I had to get Janey.” She stroked the cat, who had poked her head out of the towel and was looking around, unharmed. “She was right outside the bedroom door, crying for me.”

“I’m just glad you’re okay.” Graham felt drained.

Emma’s gaze shifted to the house, which was fully engulfed now. “Thank God, you woke up when you did,” she said. “What happened? I hadn’t been cooking or anything when you arrived.”

“I don’t think this was an ordinary cooking fire.” The blaze had been too intense, and had spread too quickly. He studied the burning house, then his gaze shifted to a trio of gas cans on the sidewalk in front of the house. “Those cans weren’t there before,” he said. As distracted and angry as he had been when he’d arrived, he would have noticed something that obvious.

Emma struggled to sit. He helped her, and

transferred the cat to her lap. Despite her ordeal, her mind remained sharp. "Someone left those cans there after they started the fire," she said. "They wanted me to know it was deliberate."

"I think you're right," he said. "And I've been so stupid. I never should have let you return to the house after the first threat." His grip tightened around her shoulder. "You could have been killed."

"We could have both been killed. Whoever did this probably knew you were with me." She nodded to his Cruiser, parked at the curb. "He—or she—was sending you a message, too."

"I'm sorry, Emma. I should have done a better job of protecting you."

"It's not your job to protect me," she said. "And I'm okay, really." She brushed her hair back out of her eyes. "Losing my home is upsetting, of course, but I'm okay. And you're okay and Janey's okay. Everything else can be replaced."

He wouldn't argue the point, but he should have protected her. "I'm going to find who did this," he said.

"I'd say you're not the only one who was ticked off by my article," she said.

He nodded. The article in the paper did

seem the most likely trigger. "The phone caller told you to stop digging into the story, and this is his way of letting you know how serious he is."

"But it also tells me I hit a nerve," she said. "If there really was no connection between Lauren Starling and Bobby Pace, I'd think whoever is behind all this would want me to pursue that angle and ignore whatever was really going on. Instead, they send me this clear indication that I'm getting too close to something they don't want the public to know."

The wail of sirens made further conversation impossible as a trio of fire trucks, followed by an ambulance, screamed onto the street. Firefighters poured out of the vehicles and swarmed the house, while a pair of paramedics headed across the lawn toward Graham and Emma.

"Is there anyone else in the house?" one of the paramedics asked.

Graham shook his head. "But you'd better check Ms. Wade. She was in the smoke for quite a while."

"I'm fine," Emma protested, but a coughing fit proved otherwise.

"We'd better check you out, and give you some oxygen to help you breathe." The pair helped her to her feet. One looked back at

Graham as they escorted Emma toward the ambulance. "You come with us, sir."

He headed after them, but veered away when he saw an older man in full bunker gear examining the trio of gas cans on the walk. The man looked up at Graham's approach. "Is this your house?" he asked, taking in Graham's half-dressed state.

"It belongs to a friend of mine," he said. No need to elaborate on his relationship with Emma; he wasn't even sure how to define it. They were lovers, certainly, but they needed more time to work out what else they were to each other. He nodded to the gas cans. "Those weren't here when I arrived this morning."

The fireman held out his hand. "Captain Will Straither," he said.

"Captain Graham Ellison, FBI." Graham shook his hand.

Straither arched one brow. "Have you made any enemies recently, Captain?"

"Then you agree the fire was likely arson?"

"We'll test for accelerants, but I'd say arson is likely. Someone wanted you to know they did this."

"Let me know what you find."

"I'd ask the same of you, Captain."

Graham nodded and headed to the ambulance, where he found both Emma and Janey inhaling oxygen, the cat with a child-size mask held to her face by one of the paramedics. "They're both going to be fine," the paramedic said as Graham approached. "We're just giving them a little oxygen to help clear their lungs."

"What about you, sir?" the second paramedic asked.

"I'm fine." Physically, he was well, at least. His mind churned with questions about what had happened, and his emotions were in turmoil.

"Then you won't mind if I check you out," the medic said.

Graham submitted to having his pulse and blood pressure checked and his lungs listened to. "You're in good shape," the paramedic said.

Emma removed her oxygen mask. Graham was glad the paramedic didn't have a stethoscope to his chest at that moment—the sight of her smiling at him definitely made his heart speed up. With her hair tousled, her face streaked with soot and her robe reduced to a dirty rag sashed over her ample frame, she was still beautiful. "I saw you talking to the fireman," she said. "What did you find out?"

"He thinks the fire was arson. They'll try to find out who did it, but I'm sure the cans won't have any prints. If we get lucky, someone might have seen a car or someone lurking around the house."

"They took a lot of risk, setting the fire during the day."

He glanced down the street, at the rows of empty driveways and curbs. "Neighborhoods like this probably have fewer people around during the day than in the evening."

"True." She leaned back against the side of the ambulance and stared at the ceiling. "What do we do now?"

"I think you and Janey should move back in with me. At least for now."

He braced himself for an argument; she was nothing if not independent. But she merely nodded. "All right. But what do we do about the case? Do you agree that someone is worried about the link I made between Bobby and Lauren?"

"I agree it's a possibility."

The dimples on either side of her mouth deepened. "I shouldn't rub it in, but I can't tell you how good it feels to have you admit you were wrong."

He bit back a sharp retort. Maybe he deserved some of her ire. "I told you I spent the morning at the airport," he said.

"Yes." She leaned forward and clasped both his hands in hers, her expression grave. "Now it's my turn to apologize for doubting you. I should have trusted you to do your job. I'm sorry."

He squeezed her hands. "I think we're two people who don't trust easily. It's going to take us time."

"I'm willing to give you time."

At that moment, he wanted more than anything to lean forward and kiss her, but he was aware of all the people around them, watching. Instead, he squeezed her hand again and leaned in, lowering his voice. "While I was at the airport, I found a pilot who says he heard Bobby arguing with someone who was in his plane with him. The pilot thinks it was a woman. He couldn't hear what they were saying, but they were both angry."

"When was this?"

"Last Monday, he thinks. And no one had seen Bobby's plane at the Montrose airport since Tuesday."

"And he was killed on Thursday."

"We're going to check some of the other airports around here, see if he flew from there between Tuesday and Thursday."

"And see if Lauren was with him."

"She may have been the woman he was arguing with at the airport Monday," Graham said. "We don't know. But I can't see how she fits into the picture. With the cargo he was carrying when he died, there was only room for one passenger. If it was Lauren, where is she now?"

"What was this mysterious cargo?" she asked.

"I can't tell you." Her expression grew stubborn, and he knew she was about to object, so he cut her off. "I really can't. It's classified."

"But whatever it is, you don't think Lauren was connected to it."

"Not unless she'd decided on a new career dealing in black-market arms—and you didn't hear that from me."

Her eyes widened. "Okay."

"If Lauren did meet with Bobby, I'm not sure that has any connection to his death the following Monday," Graham said.

"Except whoever burned down my house seems to think there's enough of a connection to warn me off. Lauren's a TV personality, but she's also a journalist. Maybe she heard about this mysterious cargo and was investigating. That led her to Bobby."

"If she got involved with the people who killed him, I'm not holding out much hope that she's still alive," he said.

"No, that doesn't seem likely. But we still need to find out what happened to her." She straightened. "I think I'll pay a visit to Richard Prentice."

The mention of the billionaire struck a jarring note. "Why would you want to talk to him?" Graham asked.

"He has connections all over the world. He might have heard something—a rumor or a hint of scandal."

"Or he might be deeply involved in all of this and going to see him could put you in even more danger," Graham said.

"I'm just going to talk to him. I can say the paper wants a follow-up story." She smiled. "You can come with me, if you like."

"He'd love that. He's suing the Rangers for harassment."

"He is? Since when?"

"Since this morning. It's another reason I was in such a foul mood when I showed up at your door."

"Then that's perfect," she said.

"How is it perfect?"

"I can say I want to talk to him about the lawsuit. But it probably wouldn't be a good idea for you to come with me."

"I don't want you going there by yourself."

"I'll be fine. I'll make sure he's aware that you and everyone at the paper know what my plans are for the day."

"Emma, I think this is a very bad idea."

Her expression sobered, and she met him with her direct, take-no-prisoners gaze. "Graham, I'm going to talk to him," she said. "You can't stop me."

Chapter Ten

The sun painted the sky in shades of gold and pink by the time the firefighters, paramedics and local police left the charred remains of Emma's home. Graham, who had spent the past hour on the phone with his team, bundled her and Janey into his Cruiser and headed for his home near the canyon. With Janey in her arms, Emma gratefully followed him inside. She set the cat on the sofa, then stretched her arms over her head. "I want a bath, clean clothes and a glass of wine—not necessarily in that order," she said.

Still shirtless, his uniform pants streaked with soot, he looked around, everywhere but at her. "We can handle all that. The big question is, where do you want to stay?"

"That depends," she said. "Where do you want me?"

His eyes met hers at last, and she felt the same, warm thrill his looks always sent through her. "I want you in my bed, but I don't want to push you. I know you like your independence."

"You're learning, Captain." She smoothed her hands down his chest, enjoying the sensation of hard muscles beneath supple flesh. She hadn't minded a bit watching him walk around shirtless most of the afternoon. "Why don't I set up Janey's things in the guest room and use it for changing, but I'll spend the nights with you."

"Sounds like a plan."

They indulged in a long, slow kiss that could have led to more, but the ringing doorbell interrupted them.

Muttering what might have been curses under his breath, Graham checked the door, then opened it.

"I got everything you asked for." Carmen Redhorse stepped into the room, her petite frame weighed down by two large shopping bags. One of the calls Graham had made was to pass along Emma's sizes and preferences and ask that Carmen make an emergency run to the store.

"Thank you so much." Emma rushed forward to take the bags, stopping to peek at the contents—underwear, shoes, tops and pants, as well as makeup and hair care products. "I pretty much got out of the house with nothing."

Carmen took in Emma's bare feet and the scorched robe cinched around her waist. She looked at her boss, who was still shirtless, her expression carefully neutral. "Do you need anything, boss?"

"Thank you, Carmen, that will be all."

She nodded and stepped back. "I'll see you later, then." She betrayed no emotion, but Emma had no doubt there would be plenty of talk back at Ranger headquarters about the captain and the reporter being caught literally with their pants down.

Carmen had also brought litter, food and other supplies for Janey. Once Emma had the cat comfortably set up in the guest room, she showered, did her hair and makeup, and put on the new clothing. Carmen had good taste, at least, and Emma felt almost human. She avoided thinking about everything she'd lost in the fire—not just clothing and jewelry and furniture, but books and pictures and other items that could never be replaced. Later on, she had no doubt the loss would hit her hard. But she couldn't let that distract her now.

She went looking for Graham and found him in his home office, seated in front of the computer at his desk. He'd showered and shaved, and wore jeans and a soft blue polo with leather moccasins. "I'm reading the article you wrote on Richard Prentice," he said.

She settled into the armchair to one side of the desk and tucked her feet up. "And?"

"You made him sound a lot more sympathetic than I would have." He swiveled the chair toward her. "I don't understand all these people who see him as some kind of hero."

"Just as many people are ready to list him as public enemy number one," she said.

"Do people admire him just because he has money?" Graham asked.

"Some of them do, and some hate him for the same reason. I think some people admire him because he flaunts authority."

"What did you think of him—really?" he asked.

She shifted. Graham wanted her to say she disliked Richard Prentice as much as he did, but she couldn't say that. "He was polite and cooperative and a gracious host," she said.

"So you liked him?" Graham asked.

"I didn't dislike him." She leaned toward him, teasing. "Are you jealous?"

His answer was a grunt. "My take is he's good at manipulating people. He saw your article as a benefit to him, so he turned on the charm. If he sees you as a threat, he could be dangerous. He may already be dangerous."

"I'm not going to be threatening," she said. "I'm going to be the reporter who wrote a wonderful profile of him and who is still on his side, while all you government types continue to persecute him."

Graham's face reddened, but he took a deep breath and relaxed a little. "I know you're just teasing me, but I don't like it."

"That's because no one ever dares to tease you," she said. "I like getting you all riled up, Captain."

"Oh, you do?" He stood and moved toward her.

She stood to meet his embrace. "Oh, I do," she said.

His kiss was more tender than she would have expected, his embrace almost gentle. She pulled back and looked into his eyes. "Hey, what is it?" she asked.

"I could have lost you." He closed his eyes and rested his forehead against hers.

"Yeah. We could have lost each other." Before they ever had a chance to find out how great they could be together. She kissed the side of his face. "Don't worry. I'm not going anywhere."

"Except into my bedroom." He took her hand and tugged her toward the door.

"I hope you've got plenty of condoms," she said.

"Guess what else Carmen bought while she was out shopping?"

"Graham, she didn't!" She wasn't one to blush, but right now her face felt as if it was on fire.

He grinned. "I'm not sure what kind of message she was trying to send, but I'll be sure to thank her tomorrow."

"You have no shame."

"Not one bit." He pulled her with him down the hall. "And right now I'm ready to pick up where we left off, before we were interrupted by that fire."

"Sleeping?"

"Just recharging. Now I'm ready to go."

"Mmm, so you are."

EMMA HAD TO use all her persuasive powers to convince Richard Prentice to grant her another interview. "Now isn't a good time," he said. "I'm very busy."

"So I've heard. I heard you're accusing The Ranger Brigade of harassment. I'd really like to hear your side of the story."

"My lawyers would advise me not to talk

to you." She pictured him seated at his ultra-modern glass-and-mahogany desk, in his home office that overlooked one end of the Black Canyon. Far different from the worn oak model in Graham's office, which she sat behind the morning after the fire, her second new computer of the week open in front of her.

"You've always been a man who followed his own counsel," she said.

He liked that; she could hear it in his voice. "Still, I think this time the attorneys may be right."

"Do you really want the public thinking you've done something wrong?" she asked.

"I haven't done anything wrong."

"Of course not, but if the Rangers are focusing their investigations on you..."

"I heard you were spending a lot of time with the Ranger captain—Ellison? The FBI guy?"

So Prentice knew about that? Should that surprise her? She and Graham hadn't exactly made a secret of their affair, so she supposed word could have gotten back to Prentice through any number of channels. Or had he been paying special attention to Graham—or to her?

"We've had a little fun together," she said. "But you know me—I'm my own woman.

I like to make up my own mind about things. I really want to hear your side of the story—and so do my readers."

"Ellison isn't sending you here to spy on me, is he?"

"No man tells me what to do." Graham might try, sometimes, but he recognized the effort was futile. "I'm a reporter. I report on stories that are newsworthy. And you are always newsworthy."

"Why now more than any other time?" he asked. Give the man credit; he wanted to know all the facts before he made a decision.

"The lawsuit is one reason, but I'd also like to know what you have to say about Bobby Pace's death. I know he flew for you sometimes."

"Pace hadn't made a flight for me for some time." The chill had definitely returned to his voice.

"Then you need to let people know that, because I've even heard rumors some people think you might have had something to do with his murder."

"Where did you hear that?"

As if she would ever reveal a source. "Oh, you know how pilots are—they sit around between flights drinking coffee and spinning wild theories."

He fell silent and she let him stew, fingers

crossed that his desire to defend himself in the press would outweigh the advice of his lawyers to keep quiet. "All right, I can give you an hour or so," he said. "Tomorrow morning. Be here at ten. I'll leave your name with the guards."

"Thank you so much. You won't regret this, I'm sure."

She dressed carefully for her meeting with the billionaire the next morning, pulling out all the stops, with new sexy red heels and a formfitting red-and-gray dress in the retro bombshell style she favored. She looked professional and sexy, a combination she was sure appealed to a man like Prentice. With Graham occupied at Ranger headquarters, she was able to make a quick getaway, driving the rental car her insurance company had provided, since her vehicle had been destroyed in the fire that consumed her house and garage.

"It's good to see you again, Ms. Wade." The guard at the ranch gate greeted her with a grin. During her many visits to the ranch while she was writing her profile of Prentice, she'd gotten to know all of the guards.

"How are you, Jack?" She gave him her brightest smile. "It's good to see you again, too."

"Mr. Prentice said to bring you on up."

She followed Jack to the front of the house where another bodyguard—a new guy whose name she didn't know—showed her into the library where Prentice liked to greet visitors.

He kept her waiting ten minutes, about what she'd expected. He liked to drive home the point that he was a busy man who was doing his visitors a great favor by making time for them. She was happy to play along, and greeted him warmly. "Mr. Prentice, thank you so much for taking time out of your busy schedule to speak with me," she said. "I really appreciate it."

He took both her hands in his and kissed her lightly on the cheek. "Only for you, Emma." He motioned to twin armchairs before the unlit fireplace. "Would you like some coffee?"

"That would be lovely."

He picked up a phone and ordered the coffee, then they settled into the chairs. If he'd been under any kind of additional strain these past few weeks, she couldn't see it in his face, which, if anything, was more relaxed than she remembered. Had he had plastic surgery? "You look happy," she said.

"I do? I suppose I am happy."

"Any special reason?"

"Do I need a reason? I mean, why wouldn't I be happy with all of this?" He spread his arms to indicate the wealth and luxury that surrounded them.

"I don't know. Forgive me for being forward, but you almost look like a man in love."

He laughed—not a mocking sound, but one of genuine contentment. "You're very perceptive," he said. "But I'm not prepared to talk about my private life today."

"Not even a hint?"

"You can say that I'm happy. That should be enough."

The coffee arrived and she waited while Richard poured and added cream and sugar to her cup—just the way she liked it. She decided to broach the subject of real interest to her. "You certainly don't look like a man who had anything to do with a murder," she said.

His expression sobered. "I was shocked to learn of Bobby's death, but as I told you on the phone, he hasn't worked for me for several weeks."

"Why is that? I assume you still need a pilot."

"Bobby was very stressed by some personal issues—his son's illness, the aftermath of his divorce. Unfortunately, that led to some behaviors that made me less willing to trust him as my pilot."

"What kind of behaviors?"

"He drank more than he should. Understandable, but drinking and flying definitely don't mix."

She'd never seen Bobby indulge in more than a couple of beers, but she couldn't claim to have known him really well. And he was under the kind of stress that drove a lot of people to self-medicate with drugs or alcohol. "Do you have any idea who he was working for when he died?" she asked.

"None. We hadn't been in contact since I told him I'd have to let him go."

"I know you're a man who has his finger on the pulse of many things. I was hoping you'd heard a rumor or gossip, maybe about someone who was looking for a pilot who would be willing to do a job that wasn't necessarily legal."

"Why do you think I would know about illegal activities?" he asked.

She smiled her most disarming smile. "Some of the people who admire you the most do so because they see you as a rebel protesting against unjust laws. Though you might not break the law yourself, some of them do, and they might tell you things, or even try to pull you into their illegal schemes, perhaps as a way of gaining cachet for their activities."

"You overestimate any contact I have

with those types of 'fans'," he said. "I abhor extremism in any form."

"So you hadn't heard any rumors about Bobby."

"Everyone knew he was desperate for money. That's probably all anyone who was looking for a pilot needed to know. But I hadn't heard of anyone in particular who needed such a pilot."

"How did Bobby take the news that you wouldn't be using him anymore?" she asked.

"He was upset, but he understood. I wished him well."

"Poor Bobby. I never knew anybody with such hard luck."

"You knew him?" Prentice's eyebrow twitched—a nervous tic she'd noted before.

"We went out a few times." She shrugged. "It was just as you said—he had a lot of personal problems, the kind of thing that leads people to drink too much. But he was a great guy. I was really wishing he'd catch a break."

"I felt the same way." He set aside his still-full coffee cup. "I've set up a fund for his boy. At least the child and his mother won't have to worry anymore about those medical bills Bobby was always struggling to pay."

"You did that for him?" She was touched, though she didn't want to show it.

He nodded. "It was the least I could do. After all, he did work for me at one time, and I make it a point to take care of my own."

"I'll be sure our readers know that." She set aside her own cup and picked up her notebook. Even though she'd set her digital recorder on the table between them, she liked to have written backup in case the electronics failed her. "So, on to this lawsuit. What have the Rangers been doing that you feel is harassment?"

"It would be easier to ask what they haven't been doing. They've come to my house several times, questioning me. Every time a crime occurs within the park, they seem to consider me as their number one suspect. They drive by my gates at all hours and fly over my property. I'm sure they have me under surveillance. Tell me, would you want to live that way?"

"No one would. Of course, that is a public road in front of your ranch gate—one that leads to the Ranger headquarters. And can you be sure the planes that fly over are theirs?"

He scowled. "Are you saying you don't believe me?"

"Not at all. But it's important for me to preserve my position as an unbiased reporter. I have to ask the tough questions and play devil's advocate, even when I don't want to." Most of the time, truth be told, she relished the role, but he didn't need to know that.

He relaxed a little. "I think it's enough to say that I have sufficient proof of harassment to justify my lawsuit."

They talked for a few more minutes, about his business interests and his long-held views against restrictions on public land and government interference in private property rights. All things she'd heard before, but she let him ramble, looking for any indication that he'd become more radical or unstable. But he seemed the same rational, if arrogant and stubborn, man she'd profiled months before.

After fifty minutes, he made a show of checking his watch. "I'm afraid we're going to have to wrap this up," he said. "I have another appointment."

"Of course. I just have a few more questions. Do you know Lauren Starling?"

He studied her, his gaze intent. "Who?"

But she was sure he'd heard her clearly. "Lauren Starling. She's the prime-time news anchor for Channel 9 in Denver. I thought you might have met her at a charity or political function. She's blonde, blue eyes—very beautiful."

"I've seen her on television. I might have

met her once or twice. It's hard to keep up. But why are you asking me about her?"

"She's missing. Her car was found several weeks ago, abandoned in Black Canyon of the Gunnison National Park. I was hoping you might have seen or heard something about her."

"I haven't heard anything. There's been nothing in the papers."

"Only a couple of smaller articles I've written." Had he really missed the front page article in which she'd theorized a connection between Lauren and Bobby? Or was he lying? "The police aren't taking her disappearance seriously. They think she might have decided to lay low for a while, or run away with a lover or something."

He smiled, though what about this news he found amusing, she couldn't imagine. "Maybe she has. The press spends too much time trying to manufacture news where there is none, and like the government, too much time prying into people's private lives." He stood. "And on that note, I really must go."

She closed her notebook and shut off her tape recorder, refusing to be baited by his rudeness. "That's all the questions I have. I think it's going to be a great article."

"Then I'll see you out."

"If you don't mind, could I use your ladies' room? It's a long way back to town."

"Of course. Down the hall and to your left."

More than a standard powder room, this bathroom featured double sinks, a steam shower and a soaking tub. A second door, which was locked, apparently led to a ground-floor guest room. Convenient if you had a guest who couldn't handle stairs, she supposed. Or maybe the locked room was a home gym and Prentice didn't like having to go all the way upstairs to shower after his workout.

She used the facilities then, telling herself it was her duty as a reporter to snoop, she checked behind the cabinet doors. She found towels, cleaning supplies and extra toilet paper in three of the cabinets, but the fourth was locked.

She stared at the lock for a long moment, then reached over and turned the water on full blast, to cover any noise she might make, and pulled a penknife from her purse. A few seconds later, she'd popped the lock and was staring at an impressive array of hairstyling products, perfume bottles and women's cosmetics, everything neatly organized in matching quilted travel bags. A carton to one side held feminine hygiene products. Emma knelt and was reaching into the cabinet to pull out one of the bags when Prentice knocked on the door. "Are you all right?" he asked.

"I'm fine. I just, uh, spilled liquid soap on my skirt and was washing it off." She pulled out her phone, snapped a picture of the contents of the cabinet, then shut the door, turned off the water and walked out to meet him.

"Sorry about that," she said.

He looked down at her skirt. "Your skirt's dry."

"I know." She smoothed her hand down her thigh. "This fabric is amazing."

He took her arm and escorted her to the door. "Goodbye, Emma." No kiss this time, only intense scrutiny, as if he was looking for some flaw in her face.

"Goodbye, Mr. Prentice. I'm sure we'll talk soon."

She climbed into her car, a little surprised that Jack or one of the other guards wasn't waiting to escort her back to the gate. But maybe Prentice figured she'd been here so many times she knew the way, and he trusted her not to stray.

She started driving, her mind a whirl. She couldn't wait to hear what Graham made of all the feminine accessories stashed in Prentice's guest bathroom. Did they belong to the mysterious new love he didn't want to talk about?

That seemed the most likely explanation—and she couldn't blame the man for wanting to keep his private life private.

Still, the reporter in her wished for something a little juicier. Maybe Prentice was a secret cross-dresser—though the feminine hygiene products didn't fit with that scenario. Maybe he had a secret mad wife in the attic—or in this case, stashed in the guest bedroom?

She shook her head, and laughed at her own wild imagination. No, the stuff probably belonged to his girlfriend, whoever she was.

She rounded a bend in the road, the house out of sight now, and pulled out her phone. She'd promised Graham she'd call to let him know she was okay. It was sweet, really, how he worried about her, though there was no need. Sure, a lot of strange things had happened in the past few days, but she was sure Richard Prentice wasn't behind them. The man had too many other things on his mind to waste his time with her.

She slowed and punched the button for Graham's number, then a hand reached around and grabbed the phone. Another hand clamped over her mouth, and then the world went black.

Chapter Eleven

"Emma? Emma!"

Graham hadn't realized he'd been shouting until Randall and Marco rushed into his office. "Something wrong, Captain?" Randall asked, amusement dancing in his hazel eyes. Ever since Carmen had reported on Graham's and Emma's nearly naked state in the middle of the afternoon—and her joke gift of a large box of condoms—Ranger headquarters had echoed with good-natured gibes at Graham's expense. "I don't think Ms. Wade is here," Randall added.

"Something's gone wrong," Graham said. "Something's happened to Emma." One minute he'd picked up the phone, elated and relieved to see her number on the screen. The next, he'd heard her low, anguished moan and a sound like screeching brakes. Then—nothing. He sank into his desk chair. He'd never admit it to his men, but his legs shook too much to hold him. If anything happened to Emma…

No. He wouldn't even think it. He had to pull himself together and help her. "She had an appointment with Richard Prentice this morning," he said, his voice steadier. "She'd agreed to call me when the interview was over. That was the call, but all I heard was a moan, then the phone went dead."

"Maybe it was just a bad connection," Randall said. "Have you tried calling her back?"

Graham snatched the phone from where he'd let it drop on his desk. He punched in Emma's number and waited for the ring. "I'm sorry, the person you are trying to reach is not available, or out of area. If you wish to leave a voice mail…"

He shoved the phone in his pocket and moved out from behind the desk. "I'm going out there," he said.

Marco grabbed him, the DEA agent's grip like an iron vise. "Not a good idea," he said.

"He already thinks we're harassing him," Randall said. "If you show up out there and Emma's all right, you'll only be adding fuel to his lawsuit."

"And if she's not all right, you won't be doing her any favors barging in on him." Marco's expression was grim.

Much as he wanted to run to Emma's rescue, he recognized the sense in his men's advice. The first rule of a hostage situation was to step back and make an assessment. Charging the scene was a recipe for disaster, especially if you weren't sure where the hostage was or what had happened. He didn't know if Emma was a hostage or not, but he wouldn't help her by rushing to her rescue without a plan.

"Is Carmen here?" he asked.

"I'm here." She must have been listening right outside the door. She joined the three men in Graham's office. "What can I do to help?"

"Call Richard Prentice and ask to speak to Emma. Tell anyone who answers that you're a girlfriend and the two of you were supposed to meet for lunch, but now you can't reach her by phone. You knew she had the interview scheduled and you need to get a message to her that you're running late."

"You want me to use my phone or yours?" she asked.

"Use one of those throwaways we keep around."

"Roger." She left the room and returned a moment later with one of the disposable pay-as-you-go phones they used when they didn't want to be easily tracked. Lotte, Randall's Belgian Malinois, followed her into the room and went to sit beside Randall, ears alert.

"She knows something's up," Randall said, smoothing his hand along the dog's side.

Carmen made the call, adding a bubbly, upbeat note to her voice that Graham hadn't heard before. In different circumstances, he would have been amused at this image of Carmen as the carefree coed, only interested in lunch and shopping. But the half of the conversation he could hear left him anything but amused.

"She's not? Are you sure? Because she definitely said she had an interview with Mr. Prentice. She was really excited about it...So her car's not there or anything...All right. Thank you. I can't imagine where she's gotten to."

She disconnected the call and met the others' worried gazes. "The guy on the phone—I think he must have been one of the bodyguards—says Emma never showed up for the interview. Mr. Prentice is very upset that she wasted his time this way."

"He's lying," Graham said. "The interview was scheduled for ten, and was supposed to last an hour. Emma called me at..." He picked up his phone and scrolled through the call log. "At eleven oh three."

"So you think whatever happened, happened as she was leaving Prentice's ranch," Randall said.

"Maybe she had a car accident," Carmen said. "Talking on the phone, a deer jumps out..." The scenario was more common than Graham wanted to admit. The combination of distracted driving and unpredictable and abundant wildlife was a recipe for numerous collisions.

"I'm going to drive out there." He started for the door once more. Emma might be lying in a ditch, unnoticed by a passerby.

"There's a quicker way to locate her," Marco said.

Graham stopped and turned to the taciturn agent. "How?"

"She was driving a rental car, right?" Marco asked.

"Yes. Her car burned up in the fire."

"What agency?" Marco pulled out his task force issued phone. "Most rentals are fitted out with LoJack, or some other locator service, in the case of an accident or theft."

"I don't know the agency, but there can't be many in a town the size of Montrose."

"When my sister's car was in the shop, her insurance company used Corporate Rentals," Carmen said.

"I'll try there first," Marco said.

He dialed the number, and put the phone on speaker, so they could all hear the conversation. Marco explained who he was and what he wanted to the young woman on the other end of the line, gave Emma's name and was transferred to a man who must have been the boss. "Come to our office at the Montrose Airport and I'll have that information for you," the man said. "I'll need to see some credentials, of course."

Graham didn't wait for more. He headed for the door, the others hurrying after him.

Marco slid into the passenger seat of Graham's Cruiser and Randall and Carmen, with Lotte in the backseat, followed in Randall's vehicle. Graham resisted the urge to head to the airport with lights and sirens, knowing this was the quickest way to pick up a trail of followers, including the press. He forced himself to keep within reasonable range of the speed limit as he raced toward town.

The manager of Corporate Rentals was waiting at the front desk with a computer printout. His already pasty face grew a shade whiter at the sight of four officers practically storming the office, but after glancing at Graham's badge, he slid the single sheet of paper across the counter. "Those are the GPS coordinates where the car has been parked for the last thirty minutes," he said.

Marco pulled out a handheld GPS unit and punched in the numbers. He angled the screen toward Graham. "That's on public land. In the Curecanti Recreation Area." The recreation area occupied forty-three thousand acres on the west side of Black Canyon of the Gunnison National Park.

"It's about a mile from Prentice's property line," Marco confirmed.

"There aren't any roads in that area," Carmen said.

The manager frowned. "The rental contract prohibits taking the vehicle off-roading," he said.

"She didn't go off-roading," Graham said. "Not voluntarily."

NO ONE SAID anything as Graham steered the Cruiser cross-country, detouring around gullies and mountains, following barely discernible trails in the rough terrain. They'd left the rental agency forty minutes before and had encountered no one since leaving the pavement.

"We should be close," Marco said, consulting the handheld GPS unit.

Graham leaned forward, scanning the landscape for anything out of place. He didn't spot the car until they were almost on it. Dust coated the once shiny red sedan, and a spiderweb of cracks spread out across the front windshield. Two tires were flat, and one front fender bowed inward.

"Looks like a rough ride," Randall said, as he and Carmen joined Graham and Marco at the front of the car.

Graham wrenched open the driver's door. The keys dangled from the ignition, and Emma's purse spilled its contents onto the passenger side floorboard. "Her phone's gone," he said, checking the contents. "So's her recorder and notebook. Her wallet's still here."

Randall let Lotte sniff the wallet. *"Sich,"* he ordered.

The dog sniffed around the car, then began following a trail, but stopped after a few dozen yards. She sat and looked back over her shoulder at Randall, whining softly.

"She got into another car and they drove away," Randall said, pointing to the faint tire tracks visible among the rocks and cacti.

"She didn't walk." Marco pointed to twin lines in the sand. "Those are drag marks. The kind that would be made by a woman's high heels."

Graham remembered the sexy red heels Emma had insisted on buying when she'd gone shopping for an outfit to wear to her interview with Prentice. "We need to get Lotte onto Prentice's ranch to look for Emma," he said. "If he took her, he's probably hiding her there."

"He'll never let us on his property," Randall said. "Not without a court order."

"He's got enough judges in his pocket that getting such an order won't be easy," Carmen said.

"We don't have time for that," Graham said.

"We could go in the back way," Marco said. "Cross-country."

"The place is crawling with guards," Carmen said. "He's practically got his own paramilitary force."

"We go in at night." Marco offered a rare grin. "With Lotte, we'll know they're there before they spot us." He nodded at the tire tracks in the dirt. "We can follow these tracks all the way to her."

Graham checked his watch. It was just after noon. "Another seven hours before dark," he said.

"That'll give us time to prepare," Marco said.

Graham only prayed they had the time, and that Emma wasn't already dead, her beautiful spirit silenced, the way Bobby Pace had been silenced. Forever.

EMMA WOKE TO a darkness so intense she thought at first she still slept, her eyes not yet open. But her other senses told her she was awake to an aching in her arms and shoulders, and a heavy throbbing in her head. The smell of earth and rocks surrounded her, with an undercurrent of a more acrid, ammonia odor. The darkness pressed in on her, frightening in its intensity. This wasn't merely nighttime, but the absence of light.

Don't panic. She repeated the words over and over, a mantra to keep the loss of control at bay. Think. What had happened? She'd been driving, talking on the phone with Graham… No, she'd been calling Graham, but she hadn't talked to him yet. Then…nothing. She had no memory beyond picking up her phone.

She was lying on a hard surface—rock hard. Her hands and feet were bound, her arms stretched painfully behind her. Carefully, she bent her knees and arched her back, trying to get a sense of the space she was in. Her feet brushed something solid—a wall, the surface uneven and hard. The source of the ammonia odor came to her—the smell of bat guano. She was in a cave, or maybe a mine.

Old shafts and exploration tunnels riddled this part of the state, a remnant of the nineteenth century gold and silver rushes.

She struggled into a sitting position, the effort making her head spin. *I must have been drugged*, she thought, as she fought a wave of nausea. She pressed her head back against a sharp protrusion of rock, welcoming the distraction of the pain.

As her head cleared, she struggled to hear any sound beyond the rasp of her own breathing. Nothing—not a drip of water or traffic noise or anything at all.

"Help!" Her shout echoed back to her, fading away into the limitless blackness. This was bad. Was someone coming back for her, or had she been left here to die?

She shuddered at the thought and struggled to stand, bracing her back against the rock and slowly, agonizingly, inching to her feet. The rock tore at her clothing and scraped her skin, but this gave her an idea. She dragged her bound wrists along the rock until the zip tie holding her caught on a jagged edge. Ignoring the pain in her shoulders, she dragged the tough nylon tie back and forth across the rock until it gave with a satisfying snap!

"Yes!" The shout rang off the rocks. She rubbed feeling back into her painful wrists and lowered herself to a sitting position once more. The ache in her swollen fingers brought tears to her eyes, but she blinked them away. She didn't have time for crying; she had to get out of here.

When she could move her fingers without crying out, she went to work undoing the bindings around her ankles. Her captors had used duct tape here, and she spent many long minutes unpicking it layer by layer.

Free at last, she stood. Being surrounded by darkness fostered a sense of vertigo, and she put out a hand to steady herself. By following the wall around, she was able to trace the outline of the chamber where she was trapped. The square room was maybe eight feet on a side. Not a cave, then, but a shaft of some kind. The walls, though rough, were slippery. Even if she took off her heels, she didn't think she could climb them, especially if she couldn't see where she was going.

She sat down again and tried not to think about how hungry and thirsty she was. Focus on the positive. She wasn't tied up anymore, and a steady current of fresh air reassured her she wasn't going to suffocate. Graham would look for her when she didn't come home. He knew she'd been going to Prentice's ranch this morning.

Had Prentice arranged for her to disappear? Had he sent one of his men after her, with instructions to shut her up? But why? She'd learned nothing in her interview that connected him to Lauren Starling's disappearance or to Bobby Pace's death. She reviewed what she could remember of their conversation, but nothing stood out. He hadn't appeared upset or concerned about any of the questions she'd asked.

Maybe someone else had attacked her after she left Prentice's home. Someone who'd followed her to the ranch and been waiting. If only she could think, but the pounding headache and painfully dry mouth interfered with her concentration.

After a while she lay on her side on the dirt floor of her prison, curled into a fetal position. She tried to sleep. Someone would come for her. She wouldn't give up hope.

Chapter Twelve

Shortly after 9:00 p.m. when the sun had fully set, Graham, Dance, Marco, Randall and Lotte set out to track Emma across the rugged terrain of the Curecanti Recreation Area. The most heavily trafficked areas of the preserve attracted hikers, campers, ATV and snowmobile riders, and fishermen. The interior land remained largely unvisited, making it the perfect place to hide illegal activity.

The Rangers wore night-vision goggles, which gave everything the eerie green glow of a video game. But this was no game. Marco led the way, keeping a shielded light fixed on the ground, following the faint impressions made by tires on the crumbly, dry surface of the prairie. Though Marco didn't have Lotte's keen sense of smell, he was the best visual tracker Graham had ever seen. He somehow picked out the subtle differences in broken grass stems and barely disturbed ground.

Even now, Graham couldn't see the tracks until Marco stopped and pointed them out to them.

Randall held the GPS. "We just crossed onto Prentice's land," he said softly.

They stopped, alert for sounds of dogs or guards. A chill breeze stirred the needles of the stunted piñons and sagebrush that dotted the ground, bringing with it the odors of dry earth and pine. An owl hooted and Graham turned in time to see the night-hunting predator lift off from the branch of a piñon on silent wings.

Marco started walking again and the others followed. Clouds obscured a quarter moon much of the time. Graham prayed he wouldn't step on a snake, then wished he hadn't thought of that.

Lotte froze, ears forward, one paw up in a pointer pose. "She's found something," Randall said. "Go on, girl. Find her." He unclipped her leash and she started off, nose to the ground. The three men followed closely, Randall taking the lead this time, just behind his dog.

Piles of rock and pieces of broken metal littered the ground around them. "Mine waste," Marco said, shining his light on a pile of bent metal strapping stained orange-red by rust.

Just ahead of them, Lotte stopped, then sat. Her excited whines sounded loud in the still darkness. "Good girl," Randall said. "What have you found?"

He stumbled on the rough ground and almost fell into what turned out to be a large hole. "Whoa!" He knelt beside the hole and looked down into it. "She's telling me there's something here, but I can't see it." He shone his light into the hole, but the darkness swallowed up the tiny beam before it penetrated the depths. "I think it's a mine tunnel."

"Not a tunnel, a ventilation shaft." Marco beamed his light onto the remains of a metal frame around the opening, then onto a massive metal grate just behind the frame. "That frame isn't as old as the rest of the metal around here. It was added later, probably as a safety precaution."

"So who moved it?" Randall shoved to his feet. "And why?"

"It would be a good place to dump a body," Graham said, fighting the cold dread growing in his stomach.

"Lotte's signaling a live find," Randall said.

Graham glanced at the dog, her gaze riveted to the shaft, tongue lolling, eyes bright. He'd heard some search and rescue dogs became depressed after finding dead bodies. Lotte didn't look depressed.

He knelt beside the shaft and cupped his hands on either side of his mouth. "Emma!" he shouted.

The cry echoed against the rock walls of the shaft. "Emma!" he called again.

"Graham? Is that you?" Emma's voice floated up to him. "Please tell me I'm not dreaming."

"You're not dreaming." He shone his light down, frustrated by his inability to see more than a few yards down. "Are you okay?"

"I'm all right. You're going to get me out of here, aren't you?"

"I'll get you out." The big question was how? They had no rope to toss down to her, no vehicle to help pull her up, no ladder to climb down.

"This shaft provides ventilation for the mine tunnels," Marco said. "The mine entrance is around here somewhere. Maybe we can reach her that way."

"You and Randall look for the entrance," Graham said. "I'll stay here with Emma." He called down to her. "Hang on. We'll get you out as soon as we can."

"Do you have any water?" she asked. "I'm really thirsty."

He pulled a bottle of water from his pack. “How far down are you? The light won’t reach.”

“A long way,” she said. “I can’t see you, either.”

“I’m going to toss down a bottle, but I don’t want to hit you.”

“There’s an opening to one side where I can stand. I think it might be the entrance to a tunnel.”

“Okay. Here comes the water.”

He dropped the bottle and listened for it to hit bottom, counting one-Mississippi, two-Mississippi… Before he’d counted two seconds he heard the bottle strike the rock below.

“I got it!” Emma called up. “Thank you!”

“It didn’t break?” he asked.

“It’s a little dented, but okay.”

“I think you’re down about sixty feet,” he said, after he worked out the math. “Are you sure you’re okay?”

“A little sore, but no broken bones or bleeding. I think I was pretty out of it when whoever it was tossed me in here.”

“What happened?”

“I don’t know. I think I was drugged.”

Hurried footsteps scuffed through the rock, coming toward him. “Randall and Marco are coming back," he said. "They must have found something."

He stood and turned to face the Rangers, but the new arrivals weren't Marco and Randall, but two strangers dressed in black. One punched Graham in the stomach and when he doubled over, the other pounded a fist on the back of his head, driving him to his knees. One good shove and he was falling, scrabbling for a hold on the sides of the shaft, the rock floor of the shaft rising up to slam into him.

GRAHAM LANDED HEAVILY at the bottom of the shaft, a single, low grunt the only sound escaping him. Emma screamed and ran to him. In the faint glow of moonlight she could just make out his form, lying awkwardly on one side, so still and silent she was afraid he was dead. "Graham." She shook him. "Graham, please."

"Emma." He opened his eyes. "Are you all right?"

"I'm fine. Better now that you're here. Are you all right?"

He grimaced, and shoved into a sitting position. "I banged up my shoulder on the way down. Maybe cracked some ribs."

"Who attacked you?" she asked.

"I don't know." He looked up and she followed his gaze to the opening of the shaft. Dark shapes appeared, blocking out what little light filtered down from the moon.

"You were warned to stay out of this!" one of the shadowy figures shouted. "You should have listened."

A narrow beam of light from a flashlight swept down into the shaft, but couldn't penetrate more than a few feet of the darkness. Graham put a finger to his lips and motioned that they should move against the wall. Emma nodded, and crawled toward the opening where a passage split off from the main shaft. She didn't want to be in the line of fire if whoever was up there started dropping rocks on them—or firing bullets.

Footsteps scuffled on the rocks far overhead, then an automobile engine roared to life. Metal clanged, and the ground shook. A horrible, screeching sound, like something heavy being dragged across rock, made her cover her ears. Then the world went black once more.

Emma gasped, and clung to Graham. Only his solid, warm presence kept her grounded in that sudden, disorienting absence of light. He put one arm around her. "They've dragged the cover back over the hole," he said.

"We're trapped." Emma shut her eyes

tightly, and pressed her face against his chest. "We're buried alive."

"Don't panic." His fingers dug into her arm. "That's what they want—for us to feel helpless. We're not helpless."

He might not be helpless, but that's exactly how she felt. She was at the bottom of a mine shaft, underground in pitch-darkness with no light or food. She'd even lost the water Graham had tossed to her. The only thing keeping her from losing her mind was the man beside her, solid and strong and calm despite the impossibility of their situation.

"I think they're gone now," he said.

"So we're alone." The words added to her despair.

"The rest of the team will look for us." He took his arm from around her and she started to protest. "I'm just taking off my pack," he said. A few seconds later, light surrounded them. She blinked in the brightness. Graham handed her the mini Maglite. "You take this. I've got another one."

She shone the flashlight around her prison. "It's not as bad as I feared," she said. No slime covered the walls, and they were alone in the chamber, with no spiders or rats or other creepy-crawlies for company. She retrieved the bottle of water from the floor and drank. "What do we do now?" she asked.

"When was the last time you ate?" he asked.

"This morning." Her stomach growled. "Yesterday morning, I guess."

"Eat this." He pressed a wrapped sandwich into her hand. "I hope you like peanut butter."

"I love peanut butter." She took a bite and almost moaned with relief.

"What happened this morning?" he asked. "At Prentice's."

"Everything was fine," she said between bites of the sandwich. "I showed up for the interview, we talked. He was his usual self, polite and businesslike. He said he stopped using Bobby as a pilot weeks ago because Bobby was drinking too much and he was worried about safety."

"Was Bobby drinking too much?"

"Not when he was with me, but we only saw each other a few times. He certainly had a lot on his mind, worries about Robby and money problems—the kind of problems that might drive a person to drink."

"And of course, Prentice didn't know anything about what Bobby had been up to since then."

"Not a thing. He did tell me he'd started

a fund to pay for Robby's medical bills. I thought that was really generous of him."

"Oh, he's generous, all right." Graham shifted, and stifled a grunt.

"Are you okay?" she asked.

"I'll be fine. What happened when you got ready to leave?"

"Nothing, really. I got in my car and started driving toward the gate. I did think it was a little unusual that he didn't have one of the guards escort me—that's the way it's always worked before. No one goes anywhere on the ranch without an escort. But I just figured they were busy, and since I'd visited so many times, Richard trusted me to see myself out."

"I answered your call, but all I heard was a cry and a sound like squealing brakes." The memory made him sick to his stomach.

"I don't remember much about the next part. I think someone in the backseat of the car grabbed me, then knocked me out—maybe with chloroform or something. I felt pretty sick when I first woke up."

"You woke up down here?"

"Yes. I was tied up, hands and feet, but I managed to cut the ties. I still felt pretty bad, so I lay down and slept, until you showed up. Thank God you did."

"I knew you had the appointment with

Prentice, and I was betting the call came while you were still here. The rental company was able to track the location of your car."

"Where was it?"

"In a gully in the Curecanti Recreation Area. A long way from any road, but not too far from Prentice's ranch. From there, Randall Knightbridge and his dog, Lotte, were able to track you to where another vehicle must have picked you up. We came back after dark and followed the tracks of that vehicle to here."

"You didn't come by yourself, I hope," she said.

"No, Randall, Michael Dance, Lotte and Marco Cruz were with me."

"What happened to them?" she asked.

"I don't know. I sent them to search for the main entrance to the mine while I waited with you." He looked up toward the ceiling. "They haven't come back yet. That's not a good sign." If the people who had thrown him and Emma down here and left them to die had killed members of his team, too, they wouldn't want to be alive when Graham got out of here.

"Maybe they're okay," she said. "Maybe they got away and went for help."

"Maybe so." He couldn't afford to dwell on

what might have happened. He had to focus on right now, and what he and Emma needed to do to survive.

She finished the last of the sandwich. "What else do you have in that magic pack?" she asked. "Maybe a phone to call for help?"

"It didn't survive the fall." He held up the phone, its screen shattered, bits of plastic hanging off it. He dropped it back into the pack and took out a flat plastic box. "I'll need you to help me fashion a sling for my shoulder and wrap my ribs. There are some bandages and gauze in this first aid kit."

She brushed crumbs from her hands. "All right. But just so you know—I never did get my first-aid badge in Girl Scouts."

"There's a booklet with diagrams in with the supplies." He began unbuttoning his shirt. "Do the ribs first."

She helped him out of the shirt, but even though she tried to be gentle, she didn't miss the sharp hiss of breath through clenched teeth as she slipped it off his injured shoulder. "Do you think it's dislocated?" she asked.

He shook his head. "Just separated. Take the gauze and wrap it as tightly as you can around my ribs."

Getting the gauze tight was easier said than

done, but after several false starts she managed to encase several inches of his torso in gauze. She pressed her lips to his chest, just above the white line of gauze, and breathed deeply of his clean, masculine scent. "Thank you for coming after me," she said. "I knew you would."

He wrapped his free arm around her. "Kiss me," he said.

"You do love to give orders, don't you, Captain?" But she kissed him, a deep, lingering kiss meant to communicate better than words how thankful she was that he was here with her.

They might have done more than kiss, but the sharp edges of the rock walls made sitting, standing and lying down uncomfortable. And Graham still needed his shoulder tended to. Reluctantly, she broke off the kiss and reached for the triangular bandage and the first aid book. "Let's see if I can figure this out," she said. "There's some ibuprofen in here, too. You should take that."

After he had washed down two ibuprofen with water, she helped him back into his shirt, then unfolded the bandage and managed to fashion a descent sling. She sat back on her heels to admire her handiwork. "Feel better?" she asked.

He nodded. "When we're out of here, I'll show you just how much I appreciate your help."

"Are we going to get out of here?" She hated the wobble in her voice, hated the panic that clawed at the back of her throat like a wild animal waiting for the chance to tear down the fragile wall of self-control she'd managed to construct. She'd always thought of herself as a strong woman, one who wasn't timid or afraid of anything.

But she'd never been in a situation like this before, attacked and buried underground by an enemy she didn't know or understand.

"We're going to get out of here." Graham sounded strong, and confident. "This shaft was dug to provide fresh air for a mine tunnel," he said. "All we have to do is find the main entrance to the mine."

And hope it wasn't blocked by rock or a steel plate, she thought, but she didn't say that. "There's a tunnel leading off from this shaft," she said.

"Then we'll start there." He slipped the strap of the pack onto his uninjured shoulder. "I'll lead the way. You can keep that light, but switch it off to save the battery. Stay close to me."

As if she needed to be told the latter. She wasn't going to let him out of touching range.

The tunnel leading away from the shaft was tall enough to walk upright for the first hundred feet or so, then narrowed so that they had to crouch, then crawl. Emma's knees ached and the rock scraped her hands, but she bit her lip and kept going. Graham wasn't complaining, so neither would she.

"I can feel air flowing past," he said. "We're on the right track."

Suddenly, crawling didn't hurt so much. She increased her speed; when she got out of this she was never going into a cave again. She might even have to avoid basements.

Graham stopped so abruptly, she bumped into him. "What is it?" she asked.

"There's a side passage here."

"Is that where we need to go?" she asked.

"It looks like someone's been using it for storage. There are a bunch of boxes and stuff."

"Has someone been using it recently?" she asked. "That could be a good sign that the entrance is still open."

"Very recently." He turned into the passage, and she followed. The tunnel opened into a rock chamber, the ceiling high enough they could stand upright once more. She massaged her aching knees and looked around, following the beam of Graham's flashlight. On first glance, it looked as if someone had been using this side tunnel as a trash dump. Rusting tin cans, old glass Coke bottles and discarded mining tools filled one corner. But as the beam of the flashlight arced across the space, Emma realized the trash had been swept aside to make room for the wooden crates and plastic tubs with lids that lined one side of the chamber, along with half a dozen red plastic gas cans. She squinted at the stenciling on the side of one of the crates. It appeared to be in a foreign language—was that Russian, or maybe Arabic?

Graham let out a low whistle. "I don't believe it," he said.

"Believe what?"

"Take a look at this."

She moved to his side and stared at the object spotlighted by his flashlight. "Is it a bomb?" It lay on its side, a six-foot-long bullet shape with four metal fins at one end.

He played the light along the sinister black shape. "I'm pretty sure it's the missile Hellfire missile we've been looking for."

Chapter Thirteen

Graham studied the missile, the pain in his shoulder and side momentarily forgotten. His hunch had been right—the cargo that had cost Bobby Pace his life had been destined for Prentice's ranch. This discovery busted his case wide-open. He'd caught the billionaire practically red-handed. No way would he be able to wriggle off the hook this time.

"Is this the mysterious cargo Bobby was carrying in his plane when he died?" Emma asked.

"This is it." He moved closer to the missile, and directed the light onto the numbers embossed on one of the tail fins. "The crate was damaged on impact, but we still have the pieces. The numbers on it should match the numbers here—and the ones in the army's records."

"Richard Prentice stole this from the army?"

"Not directly. The missile apparently went

missing some time ago. He probably purchased it on the black market."

"But...why? Is he a collector or something?"

"It's more sinister than that, I'm afraid. Rumor is, he's purchased an unmanned drone. With this missile, he can arm the drone."

"Does he plan to start his own war?"

"He already has, at least if what we believe is true—that he's the power behind the crime wave in the area. His billions have funded the meth labs and illegal grow operations, the human trafficking and artifact destruction and murders, thefts and other crimes."

"But...he's made so much money legitimately—through real estate and the companies he owns. Why risk all of that to do something illegal?"

"So he can make even more money? Crime on the scale he's operating definitely pays. Or maybe it's just an extension of his desire to gain power and defy the laws of the government he hates."

"It's unbelievable," she said.

"Not many people have wanted to believe it," he said. "But with this proof, they'll have to." He looked around the chamber. "I wish I had my phone. I'd like to take some pictures."

"Speaking of pictures, I took some interesting photos at Prentice's house." Emma rubbed her forehead. "I'd forgotten until just now."

"Pictures of what?"

"You're going to think it's silly, but at the time it seemed important."

"If you thought it was important, I'm sure it was."

"I had to use the bathroom before I left the house—we'd been drinking a lot of coffee. While I was in there, I snooped in the cabinets. Everything was normal, except one cabinet was locked, which I thought was strange."

"What was in the cabinet?"

"How do you know I opened it?" She attempted—but failed—to look indignant.

"I don't think you'd bother taking pictures of a locked bathroom cabinet."

"All right, I opened it. It was a cheap lock and it popped with no trouble."

"What was inside?"

"Makeup. Hair products. Tampons."

Definitely not the answer he'd expected. "So he has a girlfriend?"

"That's the thing—when I first arrived, I was struck by how happy and relaxed he looked. I even teased him about being in love.

He didn't deny it, but he refused to say anything more."

"Maybe he likes to keep his private life private."

"But what woman locks up all her personal stuff—and in a downstairs guest bathroom?" She shook her head. "It just seemed weird to me. And what's so special about this woman? And why does no one know about her? I read everything about the man to prepare for my initial interview with him. Except for a seven-year marriage when he was much younger, which ended in divorce, he's remained acutely single. He's photographed from time to time with various socialites or the daughters of foreign dignitaries, but there's never even a hint of a woman—or man—he might be seriously dating. I even asked him about it and he said it was because he was married to his job."

"The kind of money he has can buy the attention of almost any woman he wants, and the discretion to keep relationships silent."

"But why be so secretive?"

"It's a little strange, but it's not a crime."

"I know, but I took the pictures, anyway. And I was in there so long he knocked on the door and asked if I was all right. I wonder if, after I left, he went in there and found the broken lock. He'd have known I did it. If he was trying to hide something, he might have sent someone after me to make sure I stayed quiet."

"That's going a little far to protect the identity of a girlfriend," Graham said.

"Maybe she's married. Or famous. Or both."

"Or maybe this has nothing to do with a girlfriend." He turned back to the missile. "We've got evidence of a much bigger crime right here."

"Then why toss me down here with all this evidence?" she asked.

"Because he didn't think you'd ever get out," Graham said.

She wrapped her arms around him and laid her head on his shoulder. "If you hadn't showed up, I might have died down here."

"I don't believe that," he said. "You're too strong to merely give up. You'd have eventually made your way to the entrance." He patted her shoulder. "Which we still have to find. Come on. Let's get out of here."

Crawling through the tunnel was an agonizing process. His knees, ribs and shoulders protested with every movement. But he could still feel a strong flow of fresh air from the air shaft behind them toward some opening ahead.

After another half hour of crawling, the

tunnel widened and became taller. Graham struggled to his feet, then turned to help Emma.

"I see an opening!" she cried, and pointed ahead, where pale light streamed through a gap between the rocks.

They raced toward the opening and began clambering up a pile of rubble that half blocked the mine entrance. Emma had almost reached the top, ready to run outside, when Graham grabbed her and pulled her back, just as bullets slammed into the rocks near where her head had been seconds before.

In the ringing silence that followed, she clung to him, breathing hard. "Did you see anyone?"

"No. I just had a feeling. If I'd dumped two people in here, but I wasn't sure of their condition, I'd station a gunman outside, to pick them off when they emerged."

"That's sick."

"Does that really surprise you?"

She glanced up at the opening, longing on her face. "I guess not. So what do we do?"

He withdrew his service weapon from the holster at his side. "I can create a distraction while you make a break for it."

"But where would I go? There might be half

a dozen of them out there, waiting to grab me. Besides, if I leave, you'll be stranded."

He removed his hand from the gun. "You're right. We need to get a better idea of how many people are out there, and where they are."

"How are we going to do that?"

"I'm going to try to see out, without them seeing me." He put on the night-vision goggles, then took off the pack and dropped it at her feet. "You stay down here. I'll be right back." Keeping low, he crawled up the cascade of rubble that had either fallen, or been dumped into the mine entrance. He kept to the side of the opening, out of the moonlight, but opposite the direction from which he thought the gunfire had come. He doubted Prentice or whoever was behind this would send more than two people to babysit the cave opening, but he couldn't take the chance that he was wrong.

He lay on his stomach at the top of the opening and drew the pistol once more. Extending his arm, he squeezed off three shots in rapid succession. Then he threw himself farther to the side, out of reach of the barrage of gunfire that immediately answered his challenge. He picked up at rock and fired a fastball toward the shooters, drawing another round of fire.

He slid back down the rubble to where Emma waited, arms folded across her chest. "Since you seem to be all right, I won't waste my breath lecturing you on the foolishness of risking your life," she said.

"There's two of them, and they're both positioned under one of those pop-up shade shelters, next to a Jeep, to one side of the mine entrance. They've got a perfect view of the opening, and at that close range, even in the dark they'd mow us down with no trouble at all."

"Then why do you sound so cheerful?" she asked.

"Because—since they assume they have all the advantages, they've gotten lazy. They've positioned themselves too close to the entrance, they've lit a lantern and both of them are together, instead of spread out."

"So you're going to shoot them before they shoot you?" She shifted her gaze to the pistol.

He shook his head. "I couldn't get a good aim without presenting myself as a clear target, and they could too easily see me first and duck down behind the Jeep."

"Then what are you going to do?"

"I'm going to give them a bigger problem to think about than the two of us." He started back down the tunnel, retreating the way they'd come.

"Where are you going?" she cried, hurrying to follow him.

"I just need to retrieve a couple of things." Now that he knew where he was going, the trip down the narrow corridor didn't seem to take as long. He dragged himself along, ignoring the pain, focused on his plan. If this didn't work, he and Emma would probably both end up dead. Maybe the smart thing was to wait for help to arrive. By now the other Rangers must be looking for them.

But any moment now, the two guards under the shade canopy might grow bored with waiting and decide to come in after them. He and Emma and his pistol stood little chance against the two guards and their AR-15s. Better to risk escape while they still had a chance.

He stopped at the entrance to the storage tunnel that held the missile and began unbuttoning his shirt. "Not that I don't love the sight of you naked, Captain, but now doesn't quite seem the time," she said.

"I don't want to bother taking off the sling." He extended one arm to her. "See if you can start a tear and rip most of the shirt off me."

"This is sounding more interesting all the time. What are you planning?"

"I need the torn fabric to make a fuse."

She didn't ask "a fuse for what?" Instead, she grasped the hem of the shirt and bit at it, then ripped at the resulting small tear, splitting the shirt in half. She slid it off his shoulder and held it out to him.

"Could you tear it into strips, about an inch and a half to two inches wide?"

While she worked on the cloth, he ducked into the storage chamber and fished two glass Coke bottles from the pile of trash. Then he headed for the gas cans stashed in the corner. Grasping the nearest one, he heard the satisfying slosh of the contents. Quickly, he filled both bottles two-thirds full, then he made his way back to Emma, careful not to spill the gas.

She wrinkled her nose as he approached. "Do I smell gasoline?"

"You do." He knelt and stuffed a long strip of rag into each bottle.

"Molotov cocktails?" she asked.

"Exactly. How's your pitching arm?" he asked.

"I throw like a girl. But I was on a pretty good interleague softball team two summers ago and I held my own."

"Do you think you could throw one of these about thirty feet?"

"I could probably manage that. What am I aiming for?"

"Their Jeep. I'm going to try to pitch the other one into their shade canopy. While they're dealing with the resultant fire and explosions, we make a break for it."

"Do you have a lighter?"

"I do." He reached into his pack. "Once these are lit, we have to get rid of them fast. And be careful not to spill any gasoline on you on your way over the rubble."

"We're not in a big hurry to get up there, right?" she said. "I'll crawl carefully. And here. I'd better ditch these." She slipped off the red high heels and stuffed them into the pack. "I might want them later, but for now I'll do better without them."

He slipped the pack over his shoulder once more and, each holding a bottle, they crept back up the tunnel to the mine entrance. "You'll need to stand up to get the best trajectory," he said. "The moment right before you release the bottle is the most dangerous, when they might see you and fire. So I'll go first."

"How chivalrous."

"It's not just chivalry. I can throw harder and farther, so I don't have to move as far forward into the opening." None of that played into his reasoning, of course. But in order to protect Emma, he needed to appeal to her sense of independence and fair play. She'd appreciate logic and facts more than emotions.

"I don't know whether to be insulted or impressed that with one arm in a sling you still think you can throw farther and harder than me."

"Emma, this isn't up for debate. I'll throw my bomb, then you throw yours."

"I wasn't objecting to your orders, merely your reasoning." She stepped forward and kissed his cheek, her lips a soft caress, unexpected in the tension of the moment. "Thanks for trying to distract me," she said. "And for not getting mushy. I don't think I could take that."

"I'll save the mush for later." He stared into her eyes. If these were his last moments on earth, he couldn't think of a better last image to take with him. "We're going to get out of this," he said.

She nodded. "I trust you."

He angled his hip toward her. "The lighter's in my pocket. You're going to have to ignite the fuses."

She fished out the lighter, fumbling a little. "Sorry," she said. "My hands are shaking."

"You're doing fine. Light mine, and as soon as I've launched it, light yours, throw it and run like hell. Head right, as far away from them as you can."

"Okay." She took a deep breath. "Are you ready?"

"Ready."

The lighter flared, and she held the flame to the end of the cloth fuse. It smoldered, then caught. "Step back," he said as he raised his arm for his windup.

The bomb sailed in a perfect arc and landed on top of the shade canopy, where it exploded, raining fire down onto the two guards beneath. Graham stepped to one side and Emma moved up. She tossed underhand, but her aim was just as effective. The bomb exploded in the front seat of the Jeep.

"Run!" he shouted, and took off.

EMMA WOULD HAVE given a month's worth of chocolate for a pair of tennis shoes just then. Sharp rocks cut into her feet, and she repeatedly stumbled on the uneven ground, stubbing her toes and twisting her ankles. But terror was a powerful anesthetic, and she scarcely felt the pain as she followed Graham on an undulating course through the rock and scrub. She struggled for breath and clutched at the stitch in her side. Tears streamed down her face and one knee began to throb. But still she ran, too afraid to stop, or even to risk a look back.

After what felt like an hour, but was probably only ten minutes or so, Graham slowed and dropped down behind a large boulder. "Let's…rest…a minute," he panted.

She collapsed beside him and rested her forehead on her drawn-up knees. "What's happening back there?" she asked. "Can you see?"

"I can see the glow from the fire. They're probably trying to put it out. It doesn't look like they're following."

"But they probably will follow, eventually," she said. "We won't be that difficult to track." She looked down at her bruised, bleeding feet. "And I won't be able to go much farther without shoes," she said.

He rummaged in the backpack and pulled out a pair of thick wool socks. "Put these on. They won't help much, but they're better than nothing."

She slid on the socks. "What else do you have in that magic pack of yours?" she asked. "Any chocolate?"

"No chocolate. A space blanket, duct tape, a whistle, a mirror and fire starters. Basic survival gear."

"Socks."

"Wet feet or blisters will slow you down faster than almost anything."

"Well, I'm glad you have them. I think they'll help some."

"If things get too bad, I'll carry you," he said.

The image of Graham trying to lug her five-eleven, well-padded frame across the prairie surprised a laugh from her. "You will do no such thing. I'd be more likely to be able to carry you."

"Don't test me, Emma. A fireman's carry can be pretty uncomfortable, but effective. Don't think I won't sling you over my shoulder if I have to."

"You won't have to." She wouldn't make another complaint, and she would keep up, even if her feet fell off.

"Are you about ready to move on?" he asked. "We shouldn't stay in one place too long."

"All right." She shoved to her feet, biting her lip to keep from crying out.

"We don't have to run." He took her hand. "We can walk."

Even walking was painful, though she forced herself to keep putting one foot in front of the other without complaint. They stayed in the cover of trees and rocks as much as possible, but the added darkness made walking that much more difficult. She kept tripping over rocks and roots and she felt bruised all over. That last drink of water in the mine was a fond memory. "Where are we going?" she asked.

"We're headed for the highway. Once there, we should be able to flag someone down and call headquarters."

"How do you know which way to go?"

"I have a good sense of direction."

Of course he did. Not that she wasn't glad he was so competent, but being in a relationship with a superhero was just a little intimidating. She wasn't used to having someone who was so capable of looking after her. After so many years of relying only on herself, the idea that someone else was looking out for her unsettled her. Not that she couldn't get used to it. A little more time in his arms and she might willingly let him carry her—or at least try.

A low droning, like the buzzing of a large bee, vibrated the air around her. She looked around, but saw nothing. "What is that?" she asked.

Graham stopped and listened. "I don't know." He looked around them, then pulled her into the shelter of a group of piñons. The buzzing noise grew louder.

"Is it a glider, or something?" Emma pointed at a light in the sky. The glowing light gradually grew larger, the buzzing louder. "I know—it's one of those remote-controlled planes," she said. "My neighbor used to belong to a club for people who met every weekend to fly their planes, some of which cost thousands of dollars. Someone must have driven out here to practice their hobby. Maybe he has a phone." She started to move out from the cover of the trees, but Graham pulled her back.

"No one's going to be out here in the middle of the night flying a hobby plane." He'd fished a pair of binoculars from the pack and had them focused on the light. "Though you're right that it's remote-controlled, after a fashion." He handed her the glasses.

She studied the gray, futuristic-looking craft. She'd seen photographs in the newspaper, but surely this couldn't be. Did thirst make people hallucinate? She swallowed hard, and forced the words past her parched lips. "Is that a drone?"

Chapter Fourteen

Graham restowed the binoculars in the pack. "It's a drone," he said. More proof that Prentice was behind this. Who else in the area could afford such an exotic toy? "Instead of sending men to look for us, Prentice sent out his drone. He can use it to pinpoint our position, then send someone out to pick us off."

The drone buzzed slowly over the copse of trees that shielded them. "Can it see us down here?" Emma asked.

"Probably not, if it's just equipped with a camera. An infrared scanner could spot us, though."

"Prentice can afford all the hottest technology toys," she said. "I'm betting he sprang for the infrared."

"Whether or not it can see us, as soon as we can, we should move on," he said. "We need to find a good place to hide, and to make a stand if they come for us."

"I'm not going to cower behind some rock and let them kill me." Anger brought a flush to her pale cheeks and glittered in her eyes. "I'm sick of these people seeing me as a victim—someone they can pick off at will. I'm going to show them I'll fight back with everything I have."

"You were never a victim." He pulled her close. "You're one of the strongest women I know."

"So you're not going to tell me if I had minded my own business and let the police do their work unhampered by my badgering, I wouldn't be in this fix—and you wouldn't, either, for that matter?"

"I'd as soon try to tell water to run uphill."

"That's not how you acted when we first met. You made it plain I was the enemy."

He wanted to deny the charge, but Emma would see through the lie. "I might have thought that when we first met, but no more. You were right to push for more information, and though I didn't always agree with your methods, it's clear you've struck a nerve. Thanks to your prodding, Prentice has showed his hand. I think this case is about to break wide-open, and I owe part of the credit to you."

"You're not the only one who's big enough

to admit to a change of opinion," she said. "I've seen how hard you work, and how good you are at your job. You would have solved this case without me. I only sped things up a bit."

The buzzing of the drone increased as it made another pass. "We haven't solved anything yet," Graham said. "I'm more sure of my suspicions, but I don't have proof. But as soon as we're safe again, I'll set about getting it. Prentice and his expensive lawyers won't slip away this time."

The drone passed overhead, then headed west, away from them. Graham took his arm from around Emma. "We'd better go," he said.

He kept their course toward the road, moving as quickly as they could. Emma limped along, grim faced and in obvious pain, but uncomplaining. Her fashionable dress was streaked with dirt from the mine, the hem undone on one side and her hair a wild tangle. Most of her makeup had worn off. But her spirit and determination struck him as more beautiful than any physical perfection.

After this was all over, he'd ask her to go on vacation with him. To the beach, or a lake, where they could be alone and truly get to know each other better. Somewhere far away from drug runners and drones.

"Do you see any place to hide and make our stand?" she asked.

"No." Unfortunately, the closer they got to the main highway, the more open the terrain. The ground sloped gradually toward a valley, the coarse, gravelly soil pocked with clumps of sage and bunchgrass and the occasional spiky prickly pear. If there had ever been trees here, they'd been cut down a generation ago to build fences, houses and corrals for the ranchers who had once homesteaded the land. The almost full moon shone down like a spotlight, making him and Emma visible to anyone who might be searching for them. Their only hope was to reach the highway, and help, before their enemies found them.

"Then I think we're in trouble," Emma said. She sounded calm, but when he turned to look back at her, she'd turned sickly pale. She pointed behind her. "Someone's coming, and they're in a hurry."

Two headlights headed directly toward them. Within minutes, the vehicle would be on them, but long before that, they'd be in range of a rifle.

"Get behind me." Graham pulled her behind his back and drew his gun. If a gunman in the Jeep decided to pick them off they'd both be dead within seconds, but if their goal was to take the two of them prisoner, he might have a chance, at least, to do some damage before they were taken.

Emma's fingers dug into his unhurt shoulder. "Should we surrender?" she asked. "Ask for mercy?"

"These people haven't shown a lot of mercy so far." He tightened his grip on the weapon. "When they get closer, run," he said. "I'll hold them off as long as I can."

"Graham, that's suicide."

"Then at least I'll have died protecting someone I love." It was the closest he could come to professing his feelings for her. He hoped she didn't think the words sounded forced or phony. He meant them with all his heart, even if he would have chosen a better time to say them.

In answer, she squeezed harder and pressed her face against his back, saying nothing.

The vehicle was close enough now that he could make out that it was similar to the ones Prentice's guards drove. The glare of the headlights prevented him from seeing much, though he thought he saw the silhouette of two men, a passenger and a driver. At least one of the men was armed, the butt of the weapon braced on his thigh. Graham took careful aim. A few more seconds, and they'd be within range.

Chapter Fifteen

The vehicle skidded to a halt, just out of range of Graham's pistol. "Captain, don't shoot!" the passenger called. "It's us—we've come to save you."

"Oh my gosh!" Emma moved out from behind him. "It's Lieutenant Dance and Sergeant Cruz."

Graham holstered his weapon and followed Emma toward the Jeep. The driver—Marco Cruz—started the vehicle and met them before they'd walked more than a dozen feet. "We're sure glad to see you two," Michael said.

"This is one of Prentice's Jeeps, isn't it?" Emma asked. "And those uniforms—how—?"

"Get in and we'll explain later," Marco said. "We have to get out of here."

Emma and Graham piled in the backseat. Graham didn't need to know how these two had found him or why they were masquerading as Prentice's guards. Not now. He sagged against the seat and closed his eyes, aware for the first time in hours of a dragging fatigue.

"Are you okay, Captain?" Michael shoved a bottle of water into Graham's hand and nodded to the sling. "Should I radio ahead for an ambulance?"

"Yes," Emma said. She twisted the cap off her own water bottle and drank greedily.

"I'm not going to the hospital," Graham said.

"He's got broken ribs and a separated shoulder," she said. "He needs to be checked out."

"What about you, ma'am?" Michael asked, clearly trying not to stare at her ruined dress and wild hair.

"My feet are one big blister and I'm exhausted, but it's nothing a long bath and a good night's sleep won't help. The captain is the one I'm worried about."

"You don't need to worry about me," he said.

She patted his arm. "Humor me."

Now that the danger was past, she was back to being her bossy, independent self. But he couldn't say he didn't like it.

"How did you find us?" she asked Michael.

"We've been driving around, looking for you," Michael said. "We figured once you left the mine, you'd head for the road, so we've been searching a grid. We got lucky."

"The luck is all ours," Emma said. "I don't know how much longer we'd have lasted out there by ourselves."

"Marco, what happened after you left me at the ventilation shaft?" Graham asked.

"We got into a firefight with a couple of guards who were stationed at the mine entrance. We didn't like leaving you there, but they didn't give us much of a choice. Randall took a bullet in the arm, but he'll be okay."

"Is Lotte okay?" Graham asked.

"Yes, sir. We put together a team to try to go in again and rescue you, but by the time we got there, the place was deserted—no guards and the mine was empty. That's when we set out searching for you."

"But the Jeep and the uniforms," Emma asked. "Are they Prentice's?"

"Nah," Michael said. "We borrowed the Jeep from the sheriff's department, and the uniforms are from the local army surplus story. We figured if we were going to be driving around near Prentice's place it would be a good idea to blend in."

"Did you see anyone else while you were searching for us?" Graham asked.

"Not a soul," Michael said. "The mine looked as if no one had been near it in decades."

"Too clean." Marco spoke for the first time. "They practically sanitized the place."

"Did you see the drone?" Emma asked.

"Is that what that was?" Michael asked. "We saw something, but it was so far away, we weren't sure."

"Was it armed?" Marco asked.

"No," Graham said. "He doesn't have the missile yet. Or at least, he doesn't have it with the drone. It's stashed in a side tunnel of the mine where we were trapped." He leaned forward in the seat. "Who else is out looking for us?"

"Carmen and Simon have a Jeep like this one," Marco said.

"We need to call and let them know we've found you okay." Michael picked up the radio.

"Give me that," Graham said. "I want them to watch the mine. As soon as I can get patched up and Emma's safe, we need to go back and stake out the location. They won't want to leave the missile there, now that they know we must have spotted it."

"I'll go with you," Emma said.

"No. It's too dangerous." And he couldn't focus on his job while he was worried about her.

"You've heard of embedded reporters? I'm your embedded reporter." She glared at him, chin up, arms crossed, eyes blazing. "I haven't been through all of this to miss out on the story of my career. I promise I'll stay out of your way, but I want to be there."

Though Michael and Marco faced forward, Graham knew they were taking in every word of this conversation. He didn't want to fight with Emma, not when they'd suffered so much already. And she'd proved she could keep her head in tense situations. "You can come," he said. "But you have to stay in a vehicle until I say it's safe for you to come out."

"I love it when you try to give me orders." Her tone was teasing and sexy, sending a shiver of desire through him. She was the most aggravating, challenging, confusing woman he'd ever met.

And he didn't know how he'd made it this far without her.

WHILE THE PARAMEDICS tended to Graham, Michael found camo pants and a shirt to replace Emma's ruined dress. Marco contributed a pair of boots; he and Emma wore the same size. With blisters bandaged and fresh socks she felt, if not 100 percent, at least ready to face whatever came next. When she joined the others in the conference room, the sun was just showing over the horizon. Graham had changed into a new uniform, and a fresh black sling supported his arm. "How are you feeling?" he asked.

"I'm not up to running a marathon, but that wasn't on my to-do list for today, anyway. What about you?"

"I'm fine." He turned to the others. "Carmen and Simon report no one's returned to the mine yet, but we know they will. They can't leave the missile there now that we know about it."

"They'll probably wait until it's dark again," Michael said. "Moving it in the daylight would be risky."

"Maybe." Graham walked to the whiteboard on the wall behind him and began sketching. Emma recognized a map of the mine interior. "We want to be in place, hidden and waiting for them," he said.

"You'll go back into the mine?" Emma's stomach rolled at the thought.

"The mine is the best place to hide, to catch them with the missile," he said. "I don't want anyone later claiming they didn't know it was there."

She pressed her lips together, wanting to object, but knowing she had no right. She didn't want Graham telling her how to do her job, so she wouldn't tell him how to do his. She crossed her arms and glared at him, hoping he'd read the message in her eyes, even if she couldn't say the words. A man with busted ribs and the use of only one arm had no business going down into a hole in the ground to face people who wanted to kill him.

"Marco, I want you and Michael stationed in the mine, in the chamber with the missile." He indicated the niche along the corridor that connected the air shaft and the mine entrance. "I'll put Carmen and Simon near the entrance."

"Where will you be?" Michael asked.

"I'll be parked here, behind these rocks." He sketched in a pile of boulders, to one side of the entrance. "Emma, you'll be with me."

She let out the breath she hadn't even realized she'd been holding. As long as she was with Graham, they'd both be all right. A silly superstition maybe, but one she believed.

EMMA WAS ABLE to catch a few hours' sleep on a cot in a back room at Ranger headquarters. Graham refused to go home to sleep, so she stayed also, though she tossed and turned, worried about the night ahead. Going anywhere near Richard Prentice again frightened her, but they couldn't let him get away with whatever he had planned for that missile.

At seven, the team began gathering at headquarters. Graham briefed them again on their assignments for the evening. Rather than watch Graham as he spoke, Emma studied the faces of the team. They trusted the captain with their lives; their confidence in him showed in their attention to his words and in the determined expressions on their faces. Emma knew she could trust him, too.

Everything happened very quickly after that. They all put on body armor; after some scrambling, they unearthed a Kevlar vest that left Emma's breasts only somewhat squashed. A heavy helmet with visor was guaranteed to give her a headache, but she didn't dare complain. When Marco began handing out weapons she started to ask for one, then stopped herself. She probably couldn't hit the side of a barn, even if she could figure out how to fire a gun. Instead, she asked for the one weapon with which she was truly proficient. "I need a notebook and a pen," she said.

"What for?" Graham asked.

"I need to record everything that happens."

"So you can write about it for the paper?" He didn't look pleased with the idea.

"Yes. But think how handy an eyewitness report by a civilian might be in court later."

"Michael, there's a notebook and pens in my desk."

Thus armed, she followed the others out to the Cruisers. Graham said nothing as he drove along the paved park road, headed for Curecanti Recreation Area. Emma followed his lead and kept silent, and tried not to think of the danger that lay ahead. Instead, she focused on Richard Prentice. Was he really behind all of this? The idea of him with a gun, killing anyone, was so out of place with his businessman's image.

Then again, maybe he never actually pulled a trigger. Instead, he paid others to do his dirty work.

After half an hour, they reached the turnoff from the paved highway onto the dirt track that led across Curecanti Recreation area to the mine. They sped across the rough ground, the ride jarring and even painful, but Emma held on and said nothing. She wouldn't give Graham a reason to regret including her. Near the mine, the team split up. Michael and Marco headed across the desert, while Graham maneuvered the Cruiser behind the boulders, until it was hidden from anyone who approached the mine entrance.

He unbuckled his seat belt and Emma did the same, then they sat in silence, listening to the ping of the cooling engine. In spite of the cooling night air within seconds she was sweating under the body armor. The helmet hurt her head and her feet ached. Graham had to be feeling even worse, but he didn't show it.

"What do we do now?" she asked.

"We wait."

The silence closed around them once more. She shifted in her seat and glanced at Graham, his face impassive, gaze focused on the horizon. Did he even remember she was here? They had so much they could talk about. Where was their relationship going? Could they really make it together? Did he still see her as the enemy reporter, or had his feelings changed?

But she already knew he wasn't a talker. Under duress, he'd admitted he loved her. That would have to be enough.

The radio crackled. "We're in place in the tunnel," Cruz said. "But there's a problem."

Graham keyed the mic. "Go ahead."

"We're in the passage between the entrance and the air shaft. It's like you described it, a storage area, with boxes and gas cans. But no missile."

"Could you repeat that? I didn't copy."

"The missile's gone, Captain. They got here ahead of us."

Chapter Sixteen

Graham might have stayed at the mine all night while evidence techs combed over the tunnels and the surrounding areas, searching for any clue to the missile's whereabouts. But Emma persuaded him to take her home. He might not admit that he himself was worn-out, but he'd given in for her sake.

Janey greeted them at the door to his house, her indignant yowls letting Emma know she was not pleased by her empty supper dish. "Yes, you're so neglected," Emma cooed, cuddling the cat to her. She smiled at Graham over the top of the cat's head. "As soon as she's fed, all I want is a hot shower, a glass of wine and a bowl of soup," she said.

"You get your shower first," he said. "I'll open the wine."

"I like the way you think." As soon as Janey was purring over a bowl of Seafood Deluxe, she headed for the bedroom, stripping on her way to the shower, where she stood under the spray with her eyes closed, letting the hot water pummel away all the pain and fear of the past thirty-six hours.

She emerged from the bathroom a half hour later, hair freshly washed and blow-dried, her body shaved and moisturized and smelling of vanilla and lavender. Graham sat on the edge of the bed, a glass of wine in his hand, which he offered to her.

"You're a saint," she said as she took the wine. "My favorite person, next to whoever invented indoor plumbing. There's nothing like a hot shower for making me feel human again." She sat on the bed next to him and sipped the cold, crisp wine.

"I'll have to settle for a bath," he said. "I'm supposed to keep these bandages dry."

She caressed his uninjured shoulder. "Want some help?"

"I don't want you to think you have to play nurse."

"Who said anything about nurse?" She slid one hand beneath the open collar of his uniform shirt. "I was thinking I'd offer to scrub your back."

"I'm probably too tired for anything else."

"So am I. This will just be a nice, relaxing bath."

He slid his fingers into her hair at the back of her head. “I can’t say I wouldn’t enjoy the company.”

The master bathroom featured an oversize soaking tub in addition to the steam shower. Emma started the water, then helped Graham out of the sling and his clothes. Bandages swathed his upper torso and wrapped one shoulder. “Does it hurt much?” she asked, kissing the white cotton over his heart.

“I’ll live.”

She shut off the water when it reached his waist, then climbed in after him and picked up a washcloth and a bar of soap. “No fair,” he said. “I didn’t get to wash you,” he said.

“Maybe next time. Now close your eyes and relax.”

He submitted to her ministrations, but he kept his eyes open, his gaze as intense as a touch, caressing her bare breasts and shoulders. She washed his shoulders, arms and upper back, then transferred her attention to his stomach and hips, deliberately skipping over his very obvious erection. She set aside the washcloth in favor of her hands, caressing and stroking every inch of him, enjoying the sensuality of warm water and silken soap, and the slow burn of building desire.

He grabbed her wrist and guided her hand

to his arousal. "You're forgetting something," he said.

She stroked him, watching the passion flare in his eyes. "I thought you were tired," she teased.

"I am. Exhausted. And you still turn me on." He pulled her close, pressing her breasts against his chest, and kissed her, his mouth urgent, tongue probing. His eagerness banished her own weariness, as desire surged within her, almost overwhelming in its intensity. Water sloshed, and the soap disappeared somewhere beneath them.

"Let's get out of this tub," she said.

He stood, pulling her to her feet with him. She grabbed a towel for herself and one for him, and followed him into the bedroom. Fifteen minutes before, she'd been certain she'd fall asleep as soon as her head hit the pillow, but the reality of the man beside her trumped any dreams sleep might conjure.

They made love gently, avoiding bruises and bandages, the necessity to take things more slowly adding sweetness and tension. Graham lay back against the pillows and she straddled him, his free hand caressing the small of her back while he kissed and suckled first one breast, then another. She arched against the base of his shaft, but he pushed her away, just enough to insert one finger into her, then another, while his thumb traced lazy circles around her arousal.

She moaned, gasping for breath on the edge of control. "Do you like that?" he asked, increasing the pressure of his thumb.

"Y-yes."

Then she lost the ability to talk as he increased his tempo, his mouth returning to pull hard on one breast, and then the other. She screamed his name as her climax ripped through her, then before she had time to recover he coaxed her to raise up enough that he could slide into her, filling her and starting the spiral of desire over again.

She couldn't have said how long she rode that wave of passion, crashing to shore only to climb again. When Graham finally cried out his release along with her she was utterly spent and utterly filled. She slid alongside him and laid her head on his uninjured shoulder, his arm tight around her.

"You're supposed to be hurt," she said. "I've been so worried. I'm not used to having to think about anybody but myself and Janey, and suddenly I can't stop thinking about you. That almost feels more dangerous to me than gunfire. Do you think I'm crazy?"

When he didn't answer, she lifted her head

and studied his slack face, eyes closed, lips slightly parted. He breathed slowly and evenly, lost to the world—and to her—in sleep. She kissed his cheek and lay down once more. Maybe she was crazy. Or maybe—for the first time in a long time, or maybe forever—she was in love.

THIS IS WHAT *is must feel like to have been hit by a truck*, Graham thought. He lay in bed with his eyes closed, taking inventory of his aches and pains. Head, ribs, shoulder, legs—yep, pretty much everything hurt.

Then the scent of lavender and vanilla drifted to him, and he smiled in spite of the pain. Not everything had been bad. The end of the day had been pretty spectacular, in fact. Emma had moved him yesterday, both with her strength and bravery, and with her tenderness and passion. He'd never met another woman like her, and when he thought he'd lost her he'd felt bereft in a way he never thought possible. He wanted to show her, every moment he could, how much she'd come to mean to him.

He opened his eyes and rolled toward her, only to find her half of the bed empty. He checked the clock, which showed half past nine. He couldn't remember the last time he'd slept this late, but then again, he couldn't remember another day as eventful as yesterday. He rose and pulled on his robe, then went in search of Emma.

The aroma of coffee and the sound of tapping keys led him to his office, where he found Emma at his desk, laptop open in front of her. "Good morning," she said. Dressed in a blue silk top and jeans, her hair curling around her shoulders, she looked relaxed and content, nothing like a woman who had been knocked out, kidnapped, trapped in an abandoned mine and shot at by fleeing criminals.

"Good morning." He bent to kiss her, a long, slow embrace he hoped would persuade her to come back to bed.

She broke the contact, gently but firmly pushing him away. "You have to see what I've found," she said.

He recognized the determined gleam in her eyes. She was in work mode and there'd be no distracting her. He might as well shift gears, too. "Let me put on some clothes and grab some coffee and you can share your discovery."

"All right, but hurry. This is too good to keep to myself long."

Ten minutes later he was back at her side, dressed and caffeinated, feeling slightly less stiff and sore. He pulled a chair alongside her. "What have you got?"

"I've been researching the women in Richard Prentice's life," she said.

"You're looking for the owner of the cosmetics and other stuff in his guest bathroom."

She nodded. "It bugs me that he had the stuff locked away. And when I asked about romantic interests, he was so coy."

"I get that you're curious, but does this have anything to do with what happened yesterday?" he asked.

"Maybe. I might have ended up at the bottom of that air shaft because Prentice knew I'd found the things locked away in the bathroom. Or, I might have found another angle to explore. Take a look at this." She indicated a document on the computer screen. "This is the article from a late May issue of the *Denver Post*. Check out the photo."

The photograph that accompanied the article showed the billionaire, dressed in black tie and tails, with his arm around a slender, dark-haired beauty in a red designer gown that left little of her figure to the imagination. "Who is she?" Graham asked.

"Her name is Valentina Ferrari. According to various gossip columnists, she and Prentice were together a lot after that party."

"All right. But why should I be interested?"

"Her father is Jorge Ferrari, Venezuelan ambassador to the United States, appointed just a few months ago. For some time before that, Venezuela and the US didn't exchange ambassadors, due to strained relations. Ferrari's arrival was seen as a step forward in our relations with a country that is said to be sympathetic to terrorists. Another article I read said that Ferrari had pledged his government's cooperation in fighting suspected terrorists."

A cold chill swept through Graham. "Terrorists would love to get their hands on a Hellfire missile." He studied the photograph of Valentina, Prentice's arm around her, holding her close. "Maybe Valentina, or her father, has a connection to that missile and Prentice may or may not be in the clear."

"She could be serious about him, or she could be using him as a cover," Emma said. "Or we could be completely wrong."

"I'll put some feelers out and see if anyone in the Bureau has intel on Valentina and her dad."

"Do you have any indication Prentice is involved with the terrorists, too?" She frowned. "He didn't strike me as the type to link up with extremists. He likes to run his own show and, despite all the railing he does against government intrusion, he sees himself as a patriot."

"So do some of these jihadists. What else do you know about Valentina? Is there anything in her background to suggest she has extremist views?"

"Not really. Her mother died several years ago, so she's served as her father's official hostess. She's a part-time fashion model and has a degree in political science from NYU."

He tapped the screen. "Print me a copy of this. It may be nothing, but we'll check it out."

"It gets even more interesting." She scrolled down the page and enlarged a section of text. "Lauren Starling was at this same party. Her name is on a list of other guests, down near the bottom of the article. But it proves Prentice knew her, too."

"Maybe. Though it's possible they were both at the party and never met."

"Lauren strikes me as the type who would seek out a news-making billionaire, even if he'd somehow managed to overlook her," Emma said. "And admit it—Lauren isn't a woman many men would overlook."

The blue-eyed, blonde anchor woman would definitely turn heads, which made her disappearance all the more troubling. She wasn't the kind of woman who would easily blend into the background.

"I hadn't thought of questioning women Prentice might have associated with," he said. "It's a good idea. They would know things about him we don't. Anybody else we should look into?"

"I didn't find mention of anyone else since Valentina came onto the scene, but I did find this." She shrank the news article about the embassy gala and brought up another article, this one a small mention in the local paper. "Jorge Ferrari is coming to Colorado today—and not to Denver, but here, to Montrose."

"Why is the ambassador from Venezuela coming here?" The relatively small town wasn't a center of industry, government or education.

"The paper says he's here 'on business.' I suppose it's possible a local company has some sort of trade agreement or something with the Venezuelan government."

Graham frowned. "Is his daughter coming with him?"

"The paper doesn't mention it. Here, I printed you a copy of that article, too." She handed him a sheaf of papers, then pushed back her chair. "I think I'll head out to the airport and ask the ambassador a few questions."

"That's not a good idea," he said. "Until we know who attacked you, and why, you should stay here." He wanted her safe and out of sight.

"I'll be careful." She stood and slung her purse over one shoulder. "I had the rental car company drop off a new ride for me this morning. I'm going to stop in town and get a new phone and I'll be all set."

He rose, also. "Emma, don't be foolish," he said. "We still don't know who kidnapped you. You could still be in danger."

She set her mouth in a stubborn line he was all too familiar with. "Whoever attacked me yesterday wants me to be timid and afraid," she said. "If I stay here, hiding, I'm doing what they want. I can't let them have that kind of power over me."

"Emma, please." He tried to reign in his exasperation, but couldn't keep the edge from his voice. "I can't do my job if I'm worried about you. Whatever you have to do, it can wait until we've cleared this case and you're out of danger."

"I can't put my life on hold until you decide it's safe for me to go out!"

"And I can't let you risk your life foolishly." His voice rose to match hers.

"You can't stop me, either." She headed for the door.

"Emma, wait!"

"No, Graham. I won't wait. And you don't have any right to ask me to." She left, slamming the door behind her.

He glared at the closed door, wanting to run after her and drag her back, but knowing that would only make her angrier. Maybe he didn't have a right to ask her to stay here, where she'd be safe. But didn't the love they shared entitle him to some consideration? Was she so independent that she couldn't consider his feelings at all? Or was being independent more important than her feelings for him?

Chapter Seventeen

Fighting with Graham made Emma feel sick to her stomach. He wasn't the type to cower inside when someone was after him, so why should he expect that of her? Even if he only wanted to protect her, the best way to do that was for both of them to work toward finding out who was responsible for harassing her. Since the only two stories she'd been working on when the threats started were Bobby's Pace's murder and Lauren Starling's disappearance, solving those two mysteries should give them the answers they needed.

After a quick stop to buy a new cell phone and restore all her contacts, she drove to the airport, checking her mirrors often to make sure no one was following her. She saw nothing suspicious, and by the time she reached the airport, most of her usual confidence had returned. She'd purposely arrived earlier than the ambassador, in order to stake out a prime location and to do a little background research. She headed for Fixed Base Operations and greeted the group of men gathered in the pilot's lounge. "I hope you gentlemen can help me," she said.

"Yes, ma'am." A stocky older man stepped out from behind the counter at one end of the room and offered his hand. "Eddie Silvada, Fixed Base Operations. What can we do for you?"

"She was talking to us, Eddie," a wiry man at the table said.

"I'm sure you can all help." She took the photo of Valentina from the paper and laid it on the table. "Have any of you seen this woman here at the airport in the last week or two? Or anytime, really?"

They passed the picture around, most shaking their heads. "I think I'd remember her," the wiry man said.

"I don't remember her," Eddie said.

The man at the far end of the table, his gray hair pulled back in a ponytail, took a pair of glasses from his shirt pocket and slipped them on. He scrutinized the picture. "She wasn't this dressed up when I saw her, but I'm pretty sure it's the same woman. She was in here a couple of weeks ago. She wanted to hire a pilot."

Emma's heart sped up. "Did she give you a name?"

"She called herself Val. Sounded foreign, maybe Mexican or Spanish? She offered to pay cash, so I didn't ask too many questions."

"Why didn't you tell the police about this when they were here?" she asked.

"They wanted to know about Bobby Pace," he said. "Nobody asked if a gorgeous woman stopped by, wanting to hire a pilot."

"Where was I when this was going on?" Eddie asked.

"I don't know," he said. "Maybe you were in the bathroom."

"Did she hire Bobby Pace?" Emma asked.

"No," the man with the ponytail said. "She hired Fred Gaskin."

So much for thinking she finally had the answer she needed. "Who's Fred Gaskin?" she asked.

"He was here a little while ago." Eddie looked around, as if Fred might pop out from behind the vending machines.

"I think he's out by his plane." A younger man turned in his chair and pointed out the window, toward the airfield. "Look for a red-and-white Beechcraft, parked on the west side. Fred's got red hair—you can't miss him."

She thanked them, and hurried out the door

and across the tarmac toward the line of small planes tethered a short distance from the runway. The red-and-white Beechcraft was third in line, and a lanky man with fading red hair looked up from the engine cowling at her approach. "Can I help you?" he asked.

"Are you Fred?" She offered her hand. "I'm Emma."

He wiped his hand on his jeans before shaking hers. "What can I do for you?"

"I understand this woman hired you to fly her a couple of weeks ago." She showed him the picture of Valentina.

He studied the picture, then shook his head. "No, ma'am. You must have the wrong guy. I've never seen her before."

"But a man in there, with a gray ponytail, said she hired you." Why hadn't she stopped to get the man's name?

"Tony said that?"

"He said she came by, looking for a pilot, and he referred her to you."

He bobbed his head up and down. "I remember now. I never actually saw her—she called me on the phone. Said she needed somebody to fly her to Rhode Island for a quick trip. The plan was to stop there overnight, then come back here. You a friend of hers?"

"More of an acquaintance. When was this?"

"Hang on and I'll tell you." He walked around to the other side of the plane, leaned into the cockpit and pulled out a brown vinyl-covered day planner. He flipped through the dog-eared pages. "I talked to her on Thursday. We were supposed to fly out Saturday and come back the next day, the twentieth."

The coroner had estimated that Bobby had died on the twenty-first. If he and Val had left Montrose as planned, on Saturday the nineteenth, it was possible they'd been delayed in Newport. Or maybe they hadn't flown out until Sunday. "You said 'supposed to.' Did things not work out that way?"

"I ended up in the hospital on Friday with acute appendicitis." He made a rueful face. "I sure hated to miss out on the money, but no way could I make the trip."

"How much was she offering to pay you?"

He rubbed his hand across his jaw. "I don't know if I should say."

"Why not?"

"It might put me in a bad light. Let's just say it was a lot. More than I usually get from tourists who want a quick look around, or businessmen who need to get from one place to another in a hurry. What's it to you, anyway?"

"I'm trying to find her, that's all. Was it

enough money that you thought maybe she was doing something illegal?"

"The thought did cross my mind. She said we'd be picking up a crate with some tractor parts her cousin in Durango needed right away."

"But you didn't really think it was tractor parts?"

He shrugged. "Who offers ten thousand dollars plus expenses to fly tractor parts? Then again, what else are you gonna buy in Rhode Island?"

The smallest state in the union didn't strike Emma as a hotbed of terrorist activity, but Rhode Island was home to a major port. "When your appendix went bad, what did you do?" she asked.

"I called the number she'd given me and told her the trip was a no go. She was pretty upset. She rattled off a bunch of words in Spanish and from her tone of voice I gathered some of them weren't that nice. I gave her the numbers of some other pilots she could call who might do the work, though."

"Did one of those numbers belong to Bobby Pace?"

"Yeah." He let out a sigh. "When I heard Bobby had been shot, I wondered if it had anything to do with her."

"Why didn't you go to the police?" If he had, he might have saved them all a lot of trouble and heartache.

He held up both hands in a defensive gesture. "It wasn't really any of my business. Besides, if she was cold-blooded enough to shoot Bobby, she wouldn't think too long and hard about coming after me if she thought I'd betrayed her."

Plus, he might not get any more lucrative but possibly illegal flying jobs if word got around that he went running to the cops. "What was this woman's name?"

"All I know is Val. And before you ask, I threw away the number she gave me. Who are you, anyway? Are you a cop?"

"No. I'm a writer." But she knew a cop who would be very interested in talking to Fred. "I may need to make a quick trip to Denver soon," she said. "Do you have a card so I can get in touch with you about flying down there?"

He hesitated, then pulled a card from a pocket in the front of the day planner. "Call me. I'll give you a good rate."

"Thanks, Fred. I—"

But the rest of her words were cut off by the arrival of a sleek jet. The gleaming white fuselage dwarfed the two-and four-seat private planes tethered in sight of the runway, like an elite racing greyhound mingling with mongrels. The aircraft taxied to the end of the runway and came to a halt in front of the terminal. "Somebody with money," Fred said, raising his voice to be heard above the whine of the jet's engines. "Foreign, from the looks of that emblem on the tail."

Emma squinted at the red, blue and gold flag on the tail of the jet. She was no expert on foreign geography, but she was pretty sure the emblem indicated the plane was from Venezuela. A door to the rear of the aircraft opened and lowered to form steps leading to the tarmac. A swarthy man in a crisp navy suit and blue tie stepped out, followed by a red-faced, balding man Emma recognized from many television news stories and press conferences.

She grabbed her recorder and her notebook from her purse and raced toward the arriving dignitaries. "Ambassador Ferrari, why are you in Montrose?" she asked the darker man.

The ambassador looked down his long nose at her. "Who are you?"

"Emma Wade, with the *Denver Post*." She waved her library card in his direction. Her legitimate press pass had been destroyed in the fire at her house, but the library had been happy to issue her a new card on the spot yesterday morning when she stopped by on her way to Richard Prentice's ranch. "Do you have business locally?"

"The ambassador's business is none of your business." Senator Peter Mattheson stepped up as if to block the ambassador from Emma's view.

"Why are you traveling with the ambassador, Senator?" Emma asked.

"That's none of your business, either."

Fine. She didn't care about the blowhard senator, anyway. She turned once more to his finely dressed companion. "Ambassador Ferrari, can you tell me about your daughter's relationship with Mr. Prentice?"

"My daughter's affairs are her own concern," Ferrari said.

"Will you be seeing Mr. Prentice while you're here in Colorado?"

"I will be seeing many people while I visit your state." His smile was suave, polite and cold as ice.

"Mr. Prentice, as a concerned citizen, was kind enough to offer us any assistance he may provide while the ambassador is in Colorado," Mattheson said.

"Will Valentina Ferrari be staying at the Prentice ranch, also?" Emma asked.

"My daughter is a model," Ferrari said,

cutting off Mattheson, who had opened his mouth to declaim some more. “She has a very busy schedule. I do not expect to see her during my short visit.”

“But she is involved with Mr. Prentice?” Emma asked, pen poised over her notebook.

“No more questions.” Ferrari moved past her, head erect and shoulders stiff.

“What about Lauren Starling?” Emma called after him. “Is she a friend of your daughter’s or of Richard Prentice?”

He ignored her. Mattheson glared at her, then followed the ambassador toward the terminal.

That hadn’t given her much, except to confirm that the ambassador knew Prentice and Mattheson. And the senator and the billionaire were well-known to be working together to try to disband The Ranger Brigade. But Emma couldn’t see how this tied in with either Bobby Pace’s murder or Lauren Starling’s disappearance.

She hurried to the parking lot and slid behind the wheel of her rental in time to fall in behind the black Lexus that carried Mattheson and Ferrari. She didn’t have anywhere in particular she had to be, so she might as well follow them for a while. Maybe she’d find out what Ferrari’s mysterious business was.

He'd probably come to Montrose, Colorado, to sample the sweet corn or something like that. Sure—and Emma was going to take a cue from his daughter and be a fashion model in her next career.

By the time the Lexus turned onto the highway headed out of town, Emma was sure the senator and the ambassador were headed toward Richard Prentice's ranch. Either that, or the ambassador had a desire to see the Black Canyon of the Gunnison. They had to be aware she was behind them, but she wasn't breaking any laws, traveling on a public highway. As it happened, she had to go this way, anyway, to get to Graham's house, though she had no intention of turning off before the Lexus did.

She pulled out her new cell phone and punched the button for the camera. When the Lexus did make a move, she wanted a picture. When she called Richard Prentice to ask why the Venezuelan ambassador paid him a visit, she didn't want him to try to deny that the ambassador had been there.

The Lexus signaled a turn onto the road leading to the park, and Emma prepared to follow. But the car swerved as she made the turn, so that she had to fight to keep it on the road. Heart pounding, she guided it to the side of the road. A check of the mirrors showed the coast was clear, so she got out and checked the tires. Sure enough, the front passenger side was flat. Sighing, she pulled out her phone to call AAA. But before she could make the connection, a familiar black-and-white Cruiser slid in behind her.

Randall Knightbridge exited the Cruiser, leaving the engine running. "Car trouble?" he asked.

"A flat." She motioned to the tire.

He frowned. "Looks like a bad one. Do you have a spare?"

"I have no idea. This is a rental. They dropped it off this morning."

"Pop the trunk and let's take a look."

She opened the trunk and he took out the spare tire and tools. "This shouldn't take long," he said, rolling up his sleeves.

"Are you sure about this?" she asked. "I heard you were shot."

"Nothing serious." He indicated the bandage on his right forearm, just below a tattoo of crossed lacrosse sticks. "It was just a scratch."

"Were you following me?" she asked, as he knelt and positioned the jack under the car's frame.

"I was headed back to headquarters." He

looked up. "Why would you think I was following you?"

"Graham wasn't too happy when I left the house this morning. He thought I should stay out of sight and safe. I thought he might have asked one of you to keep an eye on me."

"No offense, ma'am, but we've got too much work to do to follow you around—even if the chief had asked. Which he didn't." He pumped the jack and the car began to rise. "What were you doing, anyway?"

"I tried to interview the ambassador from Venezuela about why he's visiting Colorado, but he didn't have much to say. Have you seen Graham this morning?"

"I saw him for a few minutes. He wasn't in a good mood." He hefted the old tire off the axle and rotated it slowly. "There's the problem." He fingered a slash in the sidewall. "Big enough to do real damage, but small enough you wouldn't discover it right away."

She leaned over him, frowning at the gash. "What caused that?"

"If I had to guess, I'd say either a pocketknife or a screwdriver. Jam it in quick, pull it out and be on your way." His eyes met hers. "The G-man's right. Someone is still out to hurt you."

She ignored the cold knot that had formed

in her stomach. “This didn’t hurt me. It just annoyed me.”

“What if I hadn’t come along right away?” He looked around them. “There’s not a lot of traffic out here. Someone else could have driven up and grabbed you. Maybe that was even their plan.”

She swallowed the bitter taste of fear. “I see your point. Are you going to tell Graham? It’ll just make him more upset.”

“I think you should be the one to tell him, not me.”

“I can’t let whoever is making these threats silence me,” she said. “I can’t let them frighten me into changing who I am.”

He shoved the spare into place and began tightening the lug nuts. “I get that.”

“I’m not sure Graham does.”

“He’s a smart guy. He’ll figure it out.”

“I hope so.” She cared about him enough to be patient. But she couldn’t keep fighting the same battle with him. She had to remain independent, to fight for what she believed in, no matter how anyone—including the man she loved—tried to stop her.

Chapter Eighteen

Graham's head ached, but he welcomed the distraction from the different kind of pain in his heart. Better not think about Emma right now; he had to focus on work. "What did we turn up at the mine yesterday?" he asked.

"Not much," Carmen said. She handed out copies of a spreadsheet. "This is an inventory of all the evidence we have that may or may not be related to Bobby Pace's death, as well as everything we've managed to compile from the fire at Emma's house and her kidnapping yesterday."

Graham frowned at the slim list under the heading *Emma*. "Not much," he said. "Not enough." The evidence in Pace's murder wasn't much better—a single thumbprint and a few partial fingerprints from the cockpit that they hadn't been able to link to Pace or anyone he knew, the spent bullet that had lodged in his chest, the busted crate from the missile and his incomplete logbook, plus lots of photographs of the body, the wrecked plane and the surrounding terrain. At the mine, they had a few mostly generic tire tracks, Emma and Graham's statements, the bullet that had wounded Lance and more photographs.

"The FAA and NTSB ruled Pace's plane crashed due to pilot error," Carmen said. "He miscalculated his approach."

"Maybe he was distracted," Michael said. "By, say, someone with a gun to his head."

"Check for a print match with a Valentina Ferrari," Graham said. "She's a Venezuelan fashion model, the daughter of the ambassador to the US."

"I'll see if I can find anything." Carmen made a note. "How does she know Bobby Pace?"

"She knows Richard Prentice. It's a long shot, but I want it checked."

The front door opened and Lotte trotted into the room, followed by Randall and Emma. Face flushed, hair windblown, she greeted him with a smile warm enough to melt a glacier. Graham wanted to pull her close and tell her how glad he was to see her but, aware of his team watching, he settled for a brief smile and a nod.

"Am I interrupting?" she asked, looking around the table.

"We're almost done." Graham motioned her toward the table. "Did you speak to Ambassador Ferrari?"

"The ambassador from Venezuela flew into Montrose this morning," she explained to the others. "I met his plane and asked questions, most of which he refused to answer. But I learned he does know Richard Prentice. In fact, I think that's who he's here to see."

"Was his daughter with him?" Graham asked.

"No, but state senator Peter Mattheson was."

The mention of the agitating senator made Graham clench his jaw. The lawmaker had made it his personal crusade to do away with The Ranger Brigade Task Force, and spouted off about it in the press at every opportunity. "What did Mattheson have to say?"

"Not much. The whole interview was pretty much a bust." She pulled out an empty folding chair beside Graham and sat. "But my visit to the airport wasn't completely wasted. Before Ferrari and Mattheson arrived, I talked to some of the private pilots. I showed them Valentina's picture and one of them recognized her. She called herself Val and tried to hire a pilot to fly her to Rhode Island about the time Bobby was murdered."

She definitely had the attention of everyone in the room now. "Did she hire Pace?" Randall asked.

"She originally hired a man named Fred Gaskin, but he came down with appendicitis the day before they were supposed to fly out. So he gave her Bobby's name."

"What would she be doing in Rhode Island?" Carmen asked.

"She told Fred she needed to pick up tractor parts for a cousin in Durango," Emma said. "So she planned to bring something back with her."

"Providence, Rhode Island, is a major port on the Atlantic," Michael said. "She could have been collecting something that had been smuggled into the country."

"Like a stolen Hellfire missile," Graham said.

"But who was the missile for?" Carmen asked. "Did Richard Prentice want to arm that drone he supposedly bought?"

"What good would it do him if he did?" Randall asked. "If he drops that anywhere, he'll attract all the wrong kind of attention and end up in a federal prison for the rest of his life."

"He's not a hothead," Emma said. "And he's definitely not stupid."

"But he has the money to buy a black-market missile," Michael said. "Maybe he's planning to frame one of the militia groups who are such fans of his. Or maybe he owes one of them a favor and this is the payback they're collecting."

"Or maybe we're looking at this all wrong," Emma said.

"What do you mean?" Graham asked.

"We know Venezuela is on the US watch list as a possible source of terrorists," she said. "What if Valentina and her father have contacts with those terrorists? Maybe they're even sympathizers?"

"And Prentice knows this and has exploited it to acquire the missile?" Michael asked.

Emma shook her head. "No. Maybe it's the other way around. Valentina is taking advantage of any feelings Prentice may have for her by persuading him to buy the missile for her."

"Most women settle for a big diamond," Carmen said.

"We don't know why she wants the missile," Emma said. "Maybe she's a true believer in the cause, or maybe she owes someone a big favor, or she's being threatened. Whatever the reason, she gets Prentice to pay for the missile, which she plans to pick up and deliver to the terrorists back in Venezuela."

"But the plane crash delayed delivery and she had to hide it in that cave," Carmen said.

"Then we found it, and she had to move it," Graham said.

"And now her father is here to pick it up and make the delivery," Michael said. "No one's going to stop and search a diplomat's plane."

"Is Ferrari with Prentice now?" Graham asked.

"I don't know," Emma said. "I was following him, but my car had a flat before I could see where they turned. Officer Knightbridge stopped to change the tire for me."

"A flat?" Graham asked, all his old worries about her safety surging forward again.

"The car with Ferrari and Mattheson turned down the road that leads to the park and to Prentice's ranch," Randall said.

Emma refused to meet Graham's gaze; he'd have to question her later. He forced his attention back to the matter at hand. "Chances are, Ferrari is at Prentice's ranch now," he said. "And I'd lay odds the missile is there, too."

"He probably wouldn't risk hiding it at the house," Carmen said.

"He put it in a mine before," Michael said.

"There are plenty of those to choose from around here."

Graham turned to the large topo map tacked to the wall behind him. The others stood and joined him around the map, studying the symbols and letters identifying features of the park and surrounding lands, including the Prentice ranch.

"There." Randall pointed to the crossed pickax symbol for a mine. "This one is closest to the ranch house. They could even have extended one of the tunnels under the house." He traced a likely path between the mine and the house with one finger.

"We need to get in there and take a look," Graham said.

"Can you get a warrant?" Cruz asked.

"Now that we have a possible terrorist connection, I think I can," Graham said. "We've got to get that missile away from there, before a lot more people get hurt."

EMMA RETREATED TO a back office, where she worked on a brief article about the ambassador's arrival in Montrose. She'd file the story before the deadline for tomorrow's paper, but she hoped by tomorrow she'd have more exciting news to report.

Shortly after noon, Graham found her. "I

thought you might like some lunch," he said, setting a paper bag with the emblem of a local sub shop on the table beside her.

"Sounds great." She opened the bag while he sat across from her with his own lunch. "How are things going for you?" she asked.

"The ambassador's pilot filed a flight plan to leave Montrose at ten this evening and fly to Houston," he said. "Our best guess is he'll file a new plan there after refueling. We've got surveillance on the ranch, but we don't expect them to make a move before dark."

"So when will you make your move?"

"We'll go in at dusk."

"I'll go with you." It wasn't a question. She looked him in the eye and he didn't look away.

"Civilians have no place on a police operation like this." He took a large bite of his sandwich.

"I'm not just any civilian. I'm the reporter who led you to the evidence that could break open this case."

She had to wait while he finished chewing. She couldn't decide if he was weighing his answer carefully, or merely stalling. "You've been helpful," he said. "That doesn't entitle you to special privileges."

"Maybe not. Does sleeping with you?" She

smiled, hoping to take some of the sting out of her words.

"That only makes me want to protect you more," he said softly.

"I'll wear a Kevlar vest, and I'll stay in the Cruiser until you tell me it's safe to leave. I won't interfere."

"Would you be able to identify Valentina Ferrari on sight?" he asked.

"I think so, yes. And Jorge Ferrari, too."

"Then that will be the official reason you're coming with us. And you'll do exactly as I say."

"Yes, sir." She gave him a mock salute, then patted his hand. "Everything will be fine, I promise."

He made a grunting sound that could have meant anything and they returned to eating their lunches. Clearly, Graham still struggled with giving her the independence she needed, but he was learning.

THE WHOLE TEAM, along with reinforcements from the Montrose County Sheriff's Department, gathered at Ranger headquarters as the sun was setting over the canyon. As the day's heat gave way to a chilly evening, Graham briefed everyone on the plan for the evening.

"We'll approach the ranch from two sides,

at the front gate and through the wilderness area," he said. "Prentice's guards will try to stop us, but we have a warrant authorizing this search. If anyone interferes, place them in custody."

He assigned teams to search the old mine and surrounding grounds for any sign of recent activity. "If you locate the missile, set a guard and notify me. Remember that anyone you encounter may be armed and dangerous, so be prepared." Though his ribs were still bandaged and Emma knew his shoulder still pained him, he'd abandoned the sling and changed into black SWAT gear, complete with a bulky Kevlar vest and riot helmet. He presented a big, commanding presence that held the attention of every man and woman in the room.

She was waiting in the front seat of the Cruiser when he led the others outside. "Afraid I'd leave you behind?" he asked as he climbed into the driver's seat.

"You would if you could," she said.

"I don't suppose I can talk you into waiting here?" he asked. "I promise to give you an exclusive when we're done."

"Nice try, but I'm coming with you. I agreed to play by your rules." She patted her chest. "I'm stuffed into this ghastly uncomfortable vest and I'm ready to duck when you give the word."

He shifted the Cruiser into gear. "Then I guess we'd better get started."

Half the vehicles fell in behind Graham on the park road while the other half, led by Randall Knightbridge and Michael Dance, set out cross-country to approach the mine from the side. The canyon itself presented a natural boundary at the rear and at the other side of the ranch, making retreat that way all but impossible.

Graham turned into the private road that led to Prentice's ranch and stopped the cruiser in front of the closed gate. His headlights cut a bright path through the gray dusk, a spotlight illuminating the empty gravel drive. She peered down the driveway, expecting to see the headlights of an approaching Jeep, but saw only darkness, only the rumble of the idling engines of the caravan behind them disturbing the evening stillness. "Have you ever been here when guards didn't greet you within a few minutes?" Graham asked.

"Never." She continued to stare down the drive. "Maybe they think if they ignore us, we'll go away."

"Do you have Prentice's number in your phone?" he asked.

"I do." She pulled her cell from her purse.

"Call him. If I try, he'll see it's me and ignore the call. But he might talk to you."

She punched in the number and listened to the series of long rings. "No answer," she said. After the tenth ring, she hung up. "What now?"

Graham keyed his radio. "Simon, bring up a pair of bolt cutters," he said. "We're going to have to go around this gate."

Ten minutes later, Simon and a man from the sheriff's department had cut the fence wire and pulled up two fence posts, opening a gap wide enough for a vehicle to easily pass through.

Graham drove to the house, which blazed with light, though no guard came out to greet them. Emma waited in the vehicle while he got out and knocked on the door. No one answered. He tried the knob, but it didn't yield.

"Do you think they're all down at the mine?" she asked. "Moving the missile?"

"Could we get so lucky?" He slid back into the driver's seat and they started forward again, leading their caravan toward the old mine site.

"I've been this way once," she said as they inched along the faint trail. "The first day I came to interview him, Prentice gave me a tour of the place. He mentioned that he planned to reopen the mine one day—that a survey had revealed it still contained gold that could be accessed with new technology."

"Do you think he was telling the truth or merely bragging?" Graham asked.

"Maybe a little of both. I've heard that with the price of gold so high, some of these mines might be worth reopening."

"Or maybe he just uses that as an excuse if anyone asks about a flurry of activity around the mine."

They rounded a sharp curve and he came to a halt and cut the lights. The vehicles behind him followed suit. "No sense giving away our presence before we have to," he said.

They inched along and gradually her eyes adjusted to the dark enough that she was able to make out the silhouettes of trees and rocks. Then the mine itself came into view—a weathered wood head frame marked the opening to the tunnel. No lights showed around this entrance, and there were no vehicles or signs of activity. Graham stopped the Cruiser, though he left the engine running. "Stay here," he told her.

She watched his flashlight beam and that of the others until they disappeared behind a tumble of rock. A half circle of moon showed just above the mountains on the horizon. In its pale light the landscape looked smudged, like a charcoal drawing. The air smelled of car exhaust and sagebrush, the only sound the occasional ping of the cooling engine. Emma hugged her arms across her stomach, adrenaline making her jittery and on edge.

A shout in the distance startled her—men's voices, followed by the heavy slam of a car door and the sharp whine of bullets ringing on metal and rock. With her heart in her throat, she clutched the door handle and strained forward, squinting into the darkness.

Footsteps pounded on the hard ground—dark figures running toward her. The driver's-side door wrenched open and Graham leaped into the driver's seat. "Hang on tight," he commanded, as the vehicle lurched forward.

"Ranger one, this is Ranger three." Carmen's voice over the radio crackled with anxiety. "What's going on? I heard gunfire."

"There's another entrance to the mine," Graham said. "A side tunnel. Or maybe this headframe is just a decoy. There are at least two vehicles back there. They took off when I surprised them. I'm going after them."

"Should we follow?" Carmen asked.

"Radio Randall and Michael. Two Jeeps headed their way, occupants armed and dangerous. We ought to be able to trap them between us. You take a team in to search the mine. They may have left someone—or something—behind."

He reached behind the seat and took a shotgun from the rack in the backseat and handed it to Emma. "Do you know how to use one of these?" he asked.

"No," she said.

"It's easy. Jack the lever." He demonstrated. "And pull the trigger. If things get bad and anyone comes near you, promise me you'll protect yourself."

She didn't know if the lump in her throat was fear, or sorrow that something might happen to Graham. If he was alive, he'd protect her, so when he said "if things get bad" what he really meant was if he wasn't around to help her. "All right." She took the weapon with shaking hands and laid it across her lap.

The Cruiser lurched forward and she clutched the shotgun so it wouldn't bounce off her knees as he headed out across the rocky ground.

She tried to calm her fears by reminding herself that when this was over, she'd have the story of her career, but all she really wanted was to be home with Janey, soaking in a hot bath and enjoying a glass of wine, not rocketing across the ground, headed for unknown danger.

"There they are!" Triumph in his voice, Graham nodded toward the faint glow of red taillights. He switched on his own lights and hit the brights. Behind him, two more Cruisers did the same.

Graham sped up, the Cruiser bouncing over the rocks, barely under control. "You're not getting any closer!" Emma shouted. "We're going to wreck."

But Graham ignored her. The vehicle ahead must have realized they were following, because it increased speed, also. Emma gave up trying to hold on to the shotgun. She let it slide to the floor and clung to the dash and the door handle, her teeth clamped together to keep them from chattering. Graham steered around cacti and boulders, through dry creek beds and over hills, the vehicle's suspension protesting with every jarring landing, engine racing.

They roared over a hill and she was surprised to discover the gap between them and the other vehicle had lessened. She thought she could make out three occupants. She was about to point this out to Graham when something pinged off the hood of the Cruiser.

"Get down!" he shouted.

She dove under the dash. "They're shooting at us!" The thought refused to register at first, but a second ping shook her back to reality and anger overtook her initial shock. "They're shooting at us!" she said again.

She grabbed the shotgun and rested the barrel on the top of the lowered side window.

"What are you doing?" Graham shouted. "Get down!"

"If you have to drive, then I have to shoot," she said. With more calm than she would ever have imagined she could possess, she levered the gun and fired.

The force of the shot propelled her back against the seat and the blast echoed in her ears. She had no idea if she'd hit anything, but she'd definitely gotten the attention of the trio in the vehicle ahead. They dove out of sight. Giddy, she prepared to shoot again.

"Emma, don't!" Graham ordered. "You might hit the missile."

She dropped the rifle as if it had suddenly heated up and burned her. "Why didn't you say something before?"

"I didn't think you'd actually shoot."

He'd slowed the vehicle and the other two Cruisers took the opportunity to catch up with them. The radio crackled. "We can surround them with a flanking maneuver," Marco said. "Michael's going to try to shoot out their tires."

Graham glanced at Emma. "I mean it this time—stay down."

She dove under the dash once more, knocking her head as the Cruiser sped up again. Closing her eyes, she tried to ignore the sound of gunfire around her.

Then, as suddenly as the violence had erupted, peace descended once more. The Cruiser rolled to a stop. The shooting had ended, replaced by the rush of the wind and the slamming of car doors. Graham left the vehicle, but Emma stayed put, though curiosity compelled her to peek out over the dash.

Graham had one of the men up against the bumper of the Jeep, cuffing his wrists, while Carmen and Michael dealt with the other two. Simon and Marco stood at the back of the Jeep, examining the bomb, the nose of which stuck out of the back window.

Assured the danger had passed, Emma sat up and unfastened her seatbelt. She was debating getting out of the Cruiser—Graham would be furious with her for disobeying his orders, but she wanted to get close enough to overhear the conversation.

The question was decided for her when the man Graham had cuffed turned to face him, cursing loudly in Spanish. He shook his head and his hat fell off, revealing a fall of long black hair and a decidedly unmasculine face. The man Graham had apprehended was no man at all, but a woman.

Emma leaped out of the Cruiser and moved forward, notebook in hand. "Who are you?" she asked.

The woman fell silent, staring at Emma. "I know you," she said after a moment, in lightly accented English. "You're that reporter. The one looking for Lauren Starling."

"Yes." In all that had happened, Emma had almost forgotten about the missing anchorwoman. "Do you know Lauren? Have you seen her?"

The woman pressed her full lips together and turned back to Graham. "I want to call my lawyer."

"You'll have plenty of time for that," Graham said. "Why don't you start by telling us your name?"

The woman lifted her chin. "My name is Valentina Ferrari. My father is—"

"Jorge Ferrari, ambassador to the US from Venezuela." Emma moved closer, ignoring Graham's frown. "You're Richard Prentice's girlfriend."

Valentina's expression grew guarded. "I am not anyone's girlfriend."

"But what a coincidence that you're now on Richard Prentice's ranch," Graham said. "With a stolen Hellfire missile in your possession. Did Prentice ask you to steal it for him?"

"I refuse to say anything else. I want to speak with my attorney, with my father and with a representative from the State Department."

"Cruz!" Graham called. "Take Ms. Ferrari to the sheriff's department and book her."

As Marco stepped forward to lead Valentina away, Graham took Emma's arm and led her back to the Cruiser. He said nothing as they fastened their seat belts and he turned the Cruiser and headed back the way they'd come. Emma looked back at the trio of vehicles. "What will happen now?" she asked.

He said nothing, guiding the vehicle over and around rocks, jaw set, eyes fixed straight ahead. If not for the tension radiating from him, Emma might have imagined he'd forgotten she was there. "Don't do this, Graham," she said.

"Don't do what?"

"Don't give me the silent treatment. I didn't do anything wrong. I didn't get out of the car until it was safe to do so." So what if he hadn't given her permission to do so yet? She was an adult, and she had a job to do, too.

He slid his hands down the steering wheel and let out a long breath. "I'm not angry with you," he said. "I'm angry with myself, for not finding a way to stop Prentice before things got this far. Now we've got a foreign national—a diplomat's daughter—involved, which means the politicians will be all over this. She'll claim diplomatic immunity and we'll have nothing."

"Will the US grant diplomatic immunity to someone who might be involved in a murder investigation?"

"It's been done before. Sometimes a country will waive diplomatic immunity, but it doesn't happen very often. Our relations with Venezuela are shaky enough right now that I don't think anyone is going to press it. Instead of finding the piece I need to solve the puzzle, the puzzle just gets bigger."

"You'll get to the bottom of this," she said. "I'll help. Maybe I can talk to her, woman to woman. Or—"

He stomped on the brake, throwing her forward. She braced against the dash as he shifted into Park and turned toward her. "Don't you think you've helped enough already?"

"Wh-what do you mean?" She stared,

wishing she could make out his features better in the darkness. All she had to gauge his emotions was the rough timbre of his voice, anger mixed with something else she couldn't identify.

"What do you think you were doing, firing that shotgun at them?" he demanded.

"You were driving and they were shooting at us. Somebody had to shoot back. Why else did you give me the gun?"

"I didn't think you'd really shoot! You said you didn't like guns."

"I don't. But I had to protect you."

He stared at her, then began to laugh. She could feel him shaking.

"What's so funny?" she asked.

"You are." He wiped his eyes. "I'm the cop. I'm the one who's supposed to protect you. Not the other way around."

"Maybe we should protect each other."

He gripped the steering wheel with his uninjured hand, his jaw working. "You know this isn't easy for me. I'm not used to a woman who's always questioning me and second-guessing my decisions."

"It's not personal, Graham. I do trust you, but I'm not used to having people tell me what to do."

"Even when it's for your own good?"

"I have to decide for myself what's for my own good," she said. "Wouldn't you feel the same way?"

"Fair enough."

"Did you mean what you said before—that you loved me?"

"Yes."

"I love you, too. Do you think that's enough for two such independent people to work together?"

She reached across the seat and he took her hand and squeezed it. "I think it's a good start," he said.

THE NEXT MORNING, Graham returned to Ranger headquarters early, only to find the rest of the team there ahead of him. "We got a match on those prints, Captain," Simon said.

Graham studied the report Simon handed him. Valentina Ferrari was a match for the previously unidentified print they'd found in Bobby Pace's plane. "That's one loose end tied up," Graham said. He dropped the paper onto his desk. "Not that it will do us much good."

"The bullet that killed Pace is the same caliber as the gun she was carrying when you arrested her," Simon said. "But ballistics isn't back with their report."

"So she killed Bobby Pace." Michael whistled. "That's cold-blooded."

"Guess looks, money and power weren't enough for her," Simon said.

Graham checked his watch. "I've got an appointment at eight to talk to Ms. Ferrari," he said. "Let's see what her story is."

"If we can't prosecute her for murder, maybe we can at least get her to incriminate Prentice," Michael said.

"He's already issued a statement to the press saying he was away last night and has no idea what Valentina was doing on his property, and no knowledge of the missile," Michael said.

"His story about being away checks out," Simon said. "He and the ambassador were at a dinner with the mayor, city council members and at least fifty other people."

Graham's stomach churned. "He's doing it again," he said.

"Doing what?" Michael asked.

"Slipping out of the net. No matter how much evidence we compile against him, he builds a story to refute it."

"So he's just a misunderstood rich guy who makes poor choices in associates," Michael said.

"He'd like us to believe that. So far, he's been doing a good job of convincing everyone else." He fished out his keys. "Come on, let's see what Valentina will tell us."

The interview room in the Montrose police station featured gray walls, gray floor, gray folding chairs and tables. A couple of ceiling mics and cameras. Nothing to distract from the business at hand.

The door opened and two deputies led in Valentina Ferrari. Dressed in baggy orange coveralls and silver handcuffs, she didn't look glamorous, but there was no denying her beauty. She lifted her chin and glared at Graham, disdain in those dark eyes.

A tall, handsome man in a gray suit only a shade lighter than his hair followed her in. "I'm Esteban Garcia," he said. "I'm Ms. Ferrari's attorney."

Graham motioned for them to sit at the table. He and Michael settled into chairs opposite them. "My client has nothing to say to you," Garcia said.

"Your client is allowed to speak for herself." Graham addressed Valentina. Without her heavy eye makeup and military clothing she looked younger, barely out of her teens. "Ms. Ferrari, how do you know Richard Prentice?"

"He is a friend of my father's."

"I have a photo here of the two of you

together, at a party at the Venezuelan consulate in Denver."

She glanced at the copy of the newspaper photo that Graham slid from a folder.

"You don't have to answer that," her lawyer said.

"It doesn't matter," she said. "He is someone my father invited to the party. He is nothing to me."

"You two look very friendly in the photo," Graham said.

Her lips curved in the hint of a haughty smile. "Men always want to be friendly with me. That doesn't mean it means anything."

Graham left the photo on the table between them and sat back. "Let's talk about the missile you were carrying in the back of the Jeep when we arrested you," he said.

"That did not belong to me."

"Then why were you helping to transport it?"

She shrugged.

"Do not say anything else," her lawyer cautioned.

Graham studied her beautiful, proud face, and he had a sudden memory of Emma, regarding him with similar defiance. The image triggered an idea. "Do you always let men like him tell you what to do?" he asked Valentina.

"I let no one tell me what to do." The words came out sharp and crisp, as if she were giving an order. "I make my own decisions."

"So were you the one who decided to buy the missile, or were you just the errand girl?" Graham hoped to trip her up, and get her to tell him the missile's intended recipient and purpose.

"I am no errand girl!"

"Right. So you bought the missile and hired Bobby Pace to fly it to Colorado for you. Then you shot him."

"I object to this line of questioning." The lawyer glared—not at Graham, but at his client, who refused to look at him.

"Let the lady answer," Graham said.

She pressed her lips together, but said nothing.

"We have your prints in the plane," Graham said. "And when ballistics gets done, we'll know the bullet that killed him came from your weapon."

"Men are so stupid," she said.

"Was Bobby Pace stupid? Is that why you shot him?"

Garcia stood. "This interview is over."

Graham waited for Valentina's answer, but

she stood and followed Garcia out of the room. Graham's phone chirped and he answered it. "Ellison."

"Ballistics says Valentina Ferrari's gun killed Bobby Pace," Simon said.

"That's one more question answered," Graham said, after he'd disconnected the call and given Michael the news. "But we still don't know what she was doing with that missile or why."

"Speaking of questions," Michael said. "I didn't want to say anything until the interview was over, but the press is outside. They want a statement."

GRAHAM FOUGHT A sense of déjà vu as he stood on the steps of the police station, facing the gathering of reporters and television cameras. He searched the eager faces for a tall, beautiful woman with red hair and generous curves, and his spirits sank when he didn't see her. Maybe Emma didn't need to attend a press conference to get the story on Valentina Ferrari, but he'd expected her to be there, if only to make sure the competition didn't scoop her. Now, he didn't have even her friendly face to help him get through this.

"Why are you holding Valentina Ferrari?"

A male reporter from one of the national papers fired the first question.

Before Graham could answer, a second reporter said, "Senator Mattheson claims the arrest of an ambassador's daughter is another example of harassment on the part of The Ranger Brigade."

"We have evidence linking Ms. Ferrari to the murder of Bobby Pace," Graham said.

"Have you formally charged her with murder?" asked a woman from the local daily.

"No charges will be filed."

Graham turned to see Senator Mattheson, flanked by the district attorney and another man in a dark suit, emerge from the police station. Mattheson stepped up beside Graham. "Ms. Ferrari will be returning to her own country this afternoon," he said. "This has all been a misunderstanding."

"Murder is more than a misunderstanding," Graham said.

The senator's gaze could have chilled meat. "Venezuela is a valued ally of the US," he said. "We will do whatever we can to protect and honor that friendship."

The press began shouting questions, their words blurring together. Graham ignored them. "Did Richard Prentice have anything to do with this?" he asked Mattheson.

He didn't know whether to be pleased or alarmed at the way Mattheson's neck reddened at the mention of the billionaire. "Mr. Prentice is a friend of the family," the senator said. "He spoke on behalf of the Ferraris." He turned to the crowd. "I think that's all we have time for today. Thank you for coming."

He started to leave, the other man in a suit following. Graham put out a hand to stop him. "Who are you?"

"Ed Stricker. State Department." The man didn't offer a hand.

"Are you one of Mattheson's buddies?" Graham asked.

"I'm the man who's trying to prevent an international incident, no thanks to you."

"So it doesn't matter to you that a man was murdered? Not to mention the question of trafficking in illegal weapons, even terrorism."

Stricker frowned. "International security takes precedence over one local murder, which we believe was an accident, anyway. As for the missile, we've taken that into custody and will be conducting our own investigation."

"You'll let me know what you find?"

"I wouldn't lose any more sleep over this, Captain." Stricker followed Mattheson back into the station.

Graham turned to the DA. "What can you tell me about this?"

"Our hands are tied," the lawyer said. "The orders came from well above my pay grade."

"So she gets away with murder."

"You can send the evidence you have to the Venezuelan authorities and they may choose to prosecute."

"I'm not holding my breath."

The DA clapped his hand on Graham's shoulder. "Let it go. There's nothing you can do now." He left to join the others.

Michael moved up alongside Graham. "Frustrating," he said.

"I don't like not having answers," Graham said. "And I don't believe Valentina Ferrari is the only one getting away with a serious crime here."

WHILE HER COMPETITION attended the press conference at the police station, Emma called every contact in her list, trying to track down anyone who could put her in touch with Valentina Ferrari. The story of a fashion model and diplomat's daughter turned murderer—and possibly terrorist—was the biggest of her career. But even more than that, she wondered if Valentina could help her find Lauren Starling. The fact that Valentina had connected Emma with the search for Lauren made Emma believe the young woman had more than a casual interest in the case. Maybe she knew something that would help.

Two calls to the Venezuelan consulate, several unanswered to Richard Prentice and one each to the State Department, Valentina's modeling agent and a foreign correspondent she'd met once at a party yielded nothing, however. She stared at the phone, out of ideas and wondering if she should have gone to the press conference, after all.

The phone rang, startling her. The screen read Unknown Number. Curious, she answered. "Hello?"

"I understand you wish to speak to me." The softly accented, feminine voice was unmistakable.

"Yes," Emma said. "I'd really like to hear your side of the story."

"I am going home to Venezuela this afternoon, but if you come to the airport now, I will give you a few minutes."

Almost giddy with excitement, Emma hung up the phone and prepared to leave. She slipped fresh batteries into her recorder and stuffed it, along with a notebook and extra pens, into her purse. She grabbed her keys, but stopped when she reached the door and pulled out her phone. She had worked alone for years, valuing that independence and the ability to shape her own fate. But maybe it was time to share this triumph with someone else.

Graham answered on the second ring. “Emma! Is everything all right?”

“Everything’s more than all right. Can you meet me at the airport in about fifteen minutes?”

“What’s going on? Are you leaving?”

“No. Just trust me and meet me at the airport. And maybe you’d better change into civilian clothes. What I’m asking you to do is very unofficial.”

He hesitated, then said. “All right. I’ll be there as soon as I can.”

Twenty minutes later they met outside the FBO. As she’d asked, he’d changed into slacks and an oxford shirt. Minus the uniform and utility belt, with no visible weapon, he looked a little less threatening, though no woman, at least, would mistake his muscular arms and broad shoulders. “What’s up?” he asked.

“Valentina Ferrari has agreed to talk to me. I thought you might like to listen in.”

“How did you manage that?”

“Persistence. And luck.” She turned toward the plane parked at the edge of the tarmac.

The Venezuelan coat of arms shone in the afternoon light. "Come on."

Two guards stopped them at the bottom of the stairs leading up to the plane. "Who is this?" one demanded, nodding to Graham.

"My bodyguard," she said. "He won't say anything. He's just here to observe."

Playing along, Graham kept quiet and allowed them to frisk him. Then one guard led the way up the stairs, while the other fell in behind.

They found Valentina alone in the luxurious cabin, dressed in designer jeans and a man's white dress shirt, unbuttoned to reveal a red silk shell and plenty of cleavage. Her feet were bare, toenails polished crimson. She studied Graham through narrow eyes. "What is he doing here?" she asked.

"Graham is only here to listen," Emma said. She was prepared to argue for him if it came to that, but Valentina merely shrugged.

She motioned for them to sit on one of the two leather sofas, then she half reclined on the other, feet tucked beneath her. "I suppose you want to talk about Bobby," she said, without preamble.

Emma took out her notebook and switched on the tape recorder. "Yes. What happened with Bobby?" she asked.

"I agreed to do a favor for...for some friends. They wanted me to pick up a...a package in Newport and fly it to Colorado."

Graham leaned forward, as if to speak, but a look from Emma silenced him. Valentina fussed with the sleeves of her shirt, carefully unrolling and rerolling them, smoothing the crease. "What happened?" Emma prompted.

"He didn't want to do the job at first. He was afraid it might be illegal, since I asked him to keep it a secret." She smiled. "I told him I was a famous Brazilian fashion model, and I was trying to avoid the paparazzi. He liked that."

"You were the woman someone heard arguing with him here at the airport," Emma said. The other pilot had gotten the day wrong, but that was an easy mistake to make.

"I suppose so. In the end, he agreed to do the job. He said he had a sick boy and needed the money. We flew to Newport the next day and everything was fine. I picked up the package and we started back here. But when we got ready to land, he became very nervous. He wanted to fly to the airport and land, instead of in the wilderness area. He was being silly." She shook her head.

"Did you shoot him?" Emma asked.

Valentina smoothed her long fingers down

her thighs, nails bright red against the dark blue denim. "It was an accident," she said softly. "I pointed the gun at him to scare him, but he lunged toward me, as if to take it from me, and it went off." She bit her bottom lip and shook her head, eyes glistening. "I didn't mean for him to die. If he'd only done what he agreed to do, nothing would have happened."

"Did Richard Prentice have anything to do with your 'package'?" Emma asked. "Was he helping you?"

"I don't want to talk about the package anymore," she said.

Emma and Graham exchanged glances. Maybe she could work the conversation back to the topic of the missile and Prentice later. "What do you want to talk about?" she asked.

"I called you because I heard you have been looking for Lauren Starling."

Emma's heart raced at the mention of Lauren, but she tried to reign in her excitement. "Do you know Lauren?" she asked. "Have you seen her?"

Valentina nodded. "We first met at the party at the embassy. She was…very sweet. Not all women are so kind to other women, especially when the other woman is younger and beautiful. She was different. She was a strong, American woman, but she was also very fragile."

"Fragile? In what way?"

Valentina shook her head. "I can't explain. She just looked…vulnerable."

"Have you seen her since the party?" Emma asked. "Do you know what happened to her?"

"I don't know." She worried her lower lip between her teeth, hesitating. Then she lifted her head and met Emma's gaze, her expression calm and determined. "But you should ask Richard Prentice that question."

"Richard Prentice knows what happened to Lauren Starling?" Emma's hand shook as she scribbled the words on her pad.

"I can't say more." Valentina stood. "You must go now. My flight will leave soon."

"Wait, no! I—" Emma rose, also, but Valentina turned her back and hurried into a rear cabin, shutting the door firmly behind her.

The two guards emerged from the shadows to escort them out of the plane once more. Graham looked as if he might resist, but Emma took his arm. "Come on. We've got everything we can here."

He waited until they were in the terminal before he spoke. "What do you make of that?" he asked.

"I think she's telling the truth," Emma

said. "About Bobby, anyway. I don't think she meant to kill him."

"She wasn't willing to incriminate Richard Prentice."

"He's a powerful man. Maybe she's afraid of him. Or maybe he's innocent."

Graham grunted. "What about Lauren Starling?"

"I think she's the real reason Valentina wanted to speak with me. I think she wants to help Lauren."

"Are you going to talk to Prentice?"

"I don't know. It might be better to do some checking around first."

He put a hand on her arm. "Be careful."

She leaned into him. "I will. I've learned my lesson. Being independent doesn't mean I have to do everything myself."

"What's the next step?" he asked.

"There are lots of next steps," she said. "As soon as the insurance pays out, I have to buy a new car, and find another house."

His eyes searched hers. "What if I made you a better offer?"

"I'm listening."

He took both her hands in his. "Do you think you could put up with a stubborn, overprotective law enforcement officer?"

"You forgot grumpy and mistrustful of the press."

He nodded. "That, too. Though there's one member of the press I've learned to trust with my life." He squeezed her hands.

She wet her suddenly dry lips. "What are you saying, Graham? I mean, do you want to keep living together or dating or..."

"I want to marry you." He slid his hands up her arms to grasp her shoulders. "No half measures. I love you. I'm asking if you love me enough to stick with me, for better or worse?"

She wasn't sure she remembered how to breathe, much less speak, but the words came out, anyway. "You won't try to smother me or change me, even when I make mistakes, or do things that drive you crazy?"

"I might try sometimes, but I won't ever fool myself into thinking you'll let my judgment trump yours. And I won't try to change you. I love you exactly the way you are."

"And I love you—bossiness, grumpiness and all."

"Is that a yes?"

"Yes, I love you. And yes, I'll marry you."

He kissed her, then brushed his knuckle along the side of her mouth. "This is either the bravest, or the craziest thing I've ever done," he said.

"It's the best thing I've ever done," she said. "You and I are going to make a great team. You just wait and see."

* * * * *